"Da!" infant Danny crowed, offering his saliva-soggy cookie to Zed.

"The child's a lefty, is he?" Zed observed a trifle uneasily.

"Like you?" Karen replied.

"As a matter of fact, I am. But what does that have to do with anything?"

Karen smiled, reached into her bag and extracted a photograph.

Zed stared in astonishment at what appeared to be a picture of himself. Except it wasn't. The man in the photo had his arm around a curvaceous redhead Zed had never seen before. He raised his eyebrows. "What's this all about?"

"Isn't it obvious?" Karen said. She nodded toward the tot…and dropped her bombshell. "This is your son."

* * *

THAT'S MY BABY!

Sometimes bringing up baby can bring surprises…and showers of love!

Dear Reader,

Happy Valentine's Day! Love is in the air, and Special Edition has plenty of little cupids to help matchmake! There are family stories here, there are breathtaking romances there—you name it, you'll find love in each and every Silhouette Special Edition.

This month we're pleased to welcome new-to-Silhouette author Angela Benson. Her debut book for Special Edition, *A Family Wedding*, is a warm, wonderful tale of friends falling in love…and a darling little girl's dream come true.

We're also proud to present Jane Toombs's dramatic tale, *Nobody's Baby*, our THAT'S MY BABY! title. Jane also has written under the pseudonym Diana Stuart, and this is her first book for Special Edition under her real name. And speaking of firsts, please welcome to Special Edition, veteran Silhouette Desire author Peggy Moreland, by reading *Rugrats and Rawhide*—a tender tale of love for this Valentine's month.

Sherryl Woods returns with a marvelous new series—THE BRIDAL PATH. Don't miss the first book, *A Ranch for Sara*, a rollicking, heartwarming love story. The second and third titles will be available in March and April! And the Valentine's Day thermostat continues to rise with Gina Wilkins's sparkling tale of opposites attracting in *The Father Next Door*.

Finally, Natalie Bishop presents readers with the perfect February title—*Valentine's Child*. This tale of love lost and then rediscovered is full of the Valentine's Day spirit!

I hope you enjoy this book, and each and every title to come!

Sincerely,

Tara Gavin, Senior Editor

Please address questions and book requests to:
Silhouette Reader Service
U.S.: 3010 Walden Ave., P.O. Box 1325, Buffalo, NY 14269
Canadian: P.O. Box 609, Fort Erie, Ont. L2A 5X3

JANE TOOMBS

NOBODY'S BABY

SPECIAL EDITION®

Published by Silhouette Books

America's Publisher of Contemporary Romance

To Barbara Faith de Covarrubias

 SILHOUETTE BOOKS

ISBN 0-373-24081-3

NOBODY'S BABY

Copyright © 1997 by Jane Toombs

This edition published by arrangement with Harlequin Books S.A.

® and TM are trademarks of Harlequin Books S.A., used under license.
Trademarks indicated with ® are registered in the United States Patent
and Trademark Office, the Canadian Trade Marks Office and in other
countries.

Printed in U.S.A.

Books by Jane Toombs

Silhouette Special Edition

Nobody's Baby #1081

Silhouette Shadows

Return to Bloodstone House #5
Dark Enchantment #12
What Waits Below #16
The Volan Curse #35
The Woman in White #51
*The Abandoned Bride #56

*Always a Bridesmaid

Previously published under the pseudonym Diana Stuart

Silhouette Special Edition

Out of a Dream #353
The Moon Pool #671

Silhouette Desire

Prime Specimen #172
Leader of the Pack #238
The Shadow Between #257

JANE TOOMBS

was born in California, raised in the upper peninsula of Michigan, and has moved from New York to Nevada as a result of falling in love with the state and a Nevadan. Jane has five children, two stepchildren and seven grandchildren. Her interests include gardening, reading and knitting.

That's My Baby!

Dear Reader,

Why is it that almost all humans, men as well as women, react to a small, helpless creature with a desire to nurture and protect? No doubt this is genetic programming for the preservation of the species, but I believe there's a spiritual side, as well.

For Mother's Day, my younger son sent me a pink ceramic plaque of his two-month-old daughter's handprint. It's hanging on the wall above my computer and I smile every time I look at the impression of that tiny hand. Little Kate is still virtually helpless but her potential is immeasurable.

Nothing in life is more uplifting and rewarding than to raise a child from an infant to an adult. Babies teach us to be unselfish, to place another's needs and welfare above our own and to find within ourselves a love that nurtures without smothering.

Besides, babies are cute, smell good—at least, most of the time!—and are wonderful to cuddle. I think holding a sleeping baby has to be one of the world's best stress relievers.

Enjoy!

Jane Toombs

Chapter One

Rosy light crept through the half-open slotted blinds of Zed Adams' bedroom—another beautiful November morning in Nevada. Zed stretched and yawned, wondering if it was ever going to rain. Or snow. Either was fine with him. He might savor the dry warmth of the day, but the ranch needed moisture of one kind or another, no doubt about it. This late in November, some kind of storm was overdue.

He slid from the bed, catching a glimpse of himself in the dresser mirror as he headed for the bathroom. He grinned, reminded of his grandmother's oft-repeated chiding when he'd been a child. "Just because we are born naked doesn't mean God intends us to remain that way."

Grandma had finally trained him to keep his clothes on, but now that he was living alone he'd reverted—at least for sleeping. And sometimes through breakfast if the day was warm. Or when he was relaxing. There was something about being naked, feeling the flow of air against his skin, that seemed right to him.

When he wandered into the kitchen, following the aroma of the coffee he'd set the timer for the night before, he checked the outdoor temperature and shrugged. Forty degrees. But it was comfortable enough inside. He'd dress later.

He yawned and unhooked a mug from the tree, the cow mug his sister had given him. "Steer clear of caffeine," it said. Having successfully convinced him to stop smoking, Jade was now waging a futile campaign against caffeine. They might have taken the lead from his gasoline but he was damned if he meant to drink unleaded coffee.

Pouring a mugful, he was savoring the first sip when he heard a car motor. Not the dual-pipes roar of Jade's four-wheel nor a pickup engine but a tinnier sound, like the motor of one of those flashy skateboards some people inexplicably favored. He glanced at the clock. Not quite seven. It was too early even for any skateboard rider he knew. Frowning, he carried the coffee with him into the living room, where he had a view of the driveway.

A skateboard, all right, a white one—with California plates, he noticed when the driver rammed on the brakes and parked by the front door. Nobody who knew him ever used the front door. A stranger—a prune-picker, at that—was invading his morning privacy. He watched the driver's door open. An attractive young woman in kneesocks, long shorts, a blazer and a small-brimmed red hat eased out, trotted around to the other side of the little car, opened that door and ducked inside.

Retrieving a briefcase, he thought with disgust. In other

words, she was selling something. It would serve her right if he opened the door exactly as he was, but then again, salespeople were hard to discourage. Reflecting that it was faintly possible she could be an auditor from the IRS—just like those guys to attack before breakfast—he made a hasty retreat to the bedroom to grab a pair of sweatpants. He was tying them at his waist as the front doorbell rang.

Scowling at having the beginning of what had promised to be a beautiful day ruined, he ran a hand through his hair and reluctantly padded to the door. He flung it open and growled, "Yes?" before actually looking at the woman.

Blinking, he gazed in stupefaction at her as well as what she carried. The baby in her arms stared solemnly back at him with wide green eyes. The woman's gaze was far from solemn. Her blue eyes fairly crackled with anger.

"Well?" she snapped. "In addition to everything else, I suppose you aren't even going to invite us in."

Temporarily at a loss for words, he stepped aside and she marched past him into the entry.

Recovering, he shut the door and said, "Ms. whoever you are, I fail to understand what this is all about."

"Of course you'd say that. I expected as much." She glanced around. "You might ask me to sit down. Danny and I would both be more comfortable."

Wordlessly he indicated the kitchen. No matter what she was up to, coffee would help him cope. She settled herself into one of his padded dinette chairs and repositioned the baby so he was sitting on her lap. He immediately began to slap the table with the palms of his hands.

"Coffee?" Zed asked, reaching for another mug, aware he'd left his own in the bedroom.

She shook her head, and her frosty "No, thank you" gave the strong impression she wasn't about to accept anything from him.

Zed poured himself a cup, sat down at the table and watched her pull some kind of a cookie from the bag she'd carried over her shoulder and put the treat into the boy's right hand. Danny transferred it to his left hand, giving Zed a momentary sense of déjà vu before he realized he was remembering himself doing the same thing as a child. Without thinking, he said, "A lefty, is he?"

"Like you?" she asked.

"As a matter of fact, I am, but what does that have to do with why you're here?"

She smiled and reached into the bag again. Extracting a photo, she offered it to him.

He took the photo from her and glanced at it, then stared in astonishment at what appeared to be a picture of himself standing on the deck of a sailboat. Except it wasn't him, because the man in the photo had his arm around a pretty and curvaceous redhead—a woman Zed had never seen before. He raised his eyebrows, shrugged and asked, "What's this all about?"

She frowned. "I figured you'd be a hard case. But don't you dare try to tell me you don't recognize Erin standing there next to you, because I know that's a lie."

He tried to give her back the photo. When she wouldn't take it, he dropped the picture onto the table. "Granted, he resembles me, but I am *not* the man in that photo. As for the redhead—Erin, did you say?—I don't recognize her for the simple reason that I've never met her. I think you'd better stop playing games and tell me who you are and why you're here."

Nodding her head toward the boy, she said, "Isn't it obvious? This is your son. Yours and Erin's. How any decent man could desert a pregnant woman—"

Zed held up a hand to halt her tirade. "Stop right there. What the hell is *your* name?"

"If you must know, I'm Erin's cousin, Karen Henderson."

"Ms. Henderson, in the first place you have the wrong man. In the second place, why are you making this accusation if the boy is your cousin's child? Why isn't this Erin here? Where's she?"

"Dead." The word seemed to echo off the kitchen walls.

Zed spread his hands. "What do you want me to say? I never knew her, so I can't grieve. Courtesy compels me to say that I'm sorry, because her death must have affected you. As for the rest, you're making a mistake."

"Da!" Danny crowed, pounding his saliva-soggy cookie on the table, where it disintegrated into mushy shreds. "Da da." He offered the tiny portion of the treat to Zed.

Taken aback by the child's wrongful accusation, Zed shook his head. "I'm not his father," he repeated. "I'm not anyone's father."

"Would you care to see the private investigator's report?" she asked.

"You mean you had a private eye check me out?" Anger roughened his voice. "Just what the hell are you up to, lady?" He shoved the photo toward her. "This is no proof. Even if the man *was* me—and it certainly is not—anyone knows photos can be faked."

Danny reached out to grab the picture, and Zed jerked

it away. The boy blinked and his lower lip began to quiver.

"Oh, hell, don't cry." Zed reached for the spoon he'd stirred his coffee with and handed it to Danny, who rewarded him with a smile, revealing two tiny lower teeth.

"That's your spoon!" Karen cried. "It's been in your mouth and has your germs on it." She tried to remove it from Danny's hand, but he gripped the spoon firmly, scowling at her. Karen gave up, saying to Zed, "I hope you don't have anything contagious."

He shook his head, wondering how he was going to rid himself of Karen Henderson. She might be attractive, but she was obviously dangerous. While he tried to think of what to do next, he grew conscious of a pervasive and very unpleasant odor.

"Oh, dear," Karen muttered. "Changing time. Where's your bathroom?"

He showed her, gave her a towel and washcloth and thankfully left her alone with the boy while she did what was necessary. Returning to the kitchen, he gulped down his cooling coffee and then picked up the photo again. The guy fascinated him. He was a dead ringer for Zed—black curly hair, same build. No matter how long he looked at Erin, though, she was still a total stranger. He didn't think the sailboat was one he'd ever been on, either.

Lifting a magnifying glass from the pen-and-memo holder by the phone, he looked through it and was able to make out the name on the boat: *Maddamti*. Completely unfamiliar—either a foreign word or some made-up cutesy name. At the far right he could see another boat, a large, many-masted one that did look familiar. Where had he seen it before? A word floated into his mind—*star*.

"Star of India!" he said aloud. That old-timer was permanently docked as a tourist attraction at the San Diego waterfront. Therefore, chances were the photo had been taken in San Diego.

He heard the click of the bathroom door opening, dropped the photo onto the table again and grappled with what to do next. He should find out what the P.I. had told Karen—if she actually had hired one, that is. Get the guy's name, that was the way to go. He was poised to ask for it when she came into the kitchen.

"I've decided what to do," she told him before he could open his mouth. "To avoid argument, I'm going to ask you to have a paternity blood test and a DNA match."

Zed stared at her unbelievingly. Was she giving up? He'd heard of blood tests that wound up neither proving nor disproving paternity, but DNA was another matter. Even if a blood test was equivocal, she couldn't possibly imagine his DNA and Danny's would come anywhere close to matching. The chances were too remote. It was the perfect way to prove her wrong and get rid of her once and for all.

"Why not?" he said. "I know I'm not the father, but, since I apparently have to convince you scientifically, I'll go along."

"And I'll come along," she said. "I can't afford to trust you not to substitute some other man."

Indignation robbed him of words.

"If you don't mind, I'll make the appointment," she continued. "If, as I expect, everything matches, you'll pay for the exam. If I should prove to be wrong, I'll pay. I believe that's fair." She paused for a moment. "Reno's the closest city of any size, right? I'll try there first. We can always travel to Sacramento if we have to.''

The urge to lay her low with a few choice phrases was almost irresistible. He clamped his jaw shut to prevent an outburst. Letting her have her way would get her out of his hair, so he'd do his best to tolerate her blasted bossiness until the tests proved her wrong.

"Deal," he muttered through clenched teeth.

She smiled, a sweet, utterly false smile. "I don't mind if you want to bring along your lawyer," she said.

"What is it you do in your spare time?" he asked, unable to resist one dig. "I mean, when you're not hassling innocent men."

"I'm a teacher. And you're not innocent." She hoisted Danny farther up onto her shoulder and started for the door. "I left his dirty diaper in your bathroom," she said. "They're disposable, but you really can't flush them down a toilet." Again she flashed the false smile. "You'll have to get used to disposing of dirty diapers sooner or later, so I figured this was a good time to start. I'll call you when the appointment is set up."

He opened the door for her and shut it after her with relief, then listened for the sound of her car departing. When he was sure she was gone, he picked up the phone and punched in Jade's home number.

"Northern Nevada Well Drilling," she said on the other end.

Why his sister couldn't leave her work at the office and relax at home was beyond him. She literally lived for the drilling—something he couldn't understand, since he'd hated the work before he bailed out.

"Got a small problem here," he told her, and described his morning so far.

"The testing sounds like a good idea to me," Jade said when he finished. "It'll solve the problem once and for all, right?"

Trust Jade to go to the heart of the matter. "No sympathy for a falsely accused brother?" he asked plaintively.

"I know you wouldn't do anything so rotten," she replied. "Maybe you ought to consult your lawyer, though."

"I'd rather keep this in the family. Once the test results are in it's a cinch she won't take it to court, so I won't need a lawyer."

"Whatever," Jade said. "Still, she does sound like a nutcase. Maybe I ought to go along for the appointment."

"*Two* bossy women? Forget it."

"Call me after you get the results, then. And good luck."

"Good luck? What do I need luck for?"

"The Paiutes say there's a trickster out there who specializes in messing you up just for fun. So we all need luck, don't we?"

"Jade, I'm not a Paiute. And neither are you."

"True, brother mine. But that doesn't mean the trickster doesn't exist and that you shouldn't watch out for him."

He hung up smiling. He and Jade had always faced the world together. Even their fights as kids hadn't broken their bond. He thought they were probably closer than most siblings, maybe because they'd been raised by their maternal grandparents who, though loving, hadn't really understood either of them. With his grandparents gone now, it was literally Jade and Zed against the world.

Jade was a volunteer in a program that provided role models for disadvantaged children, but instead of being a big sister to a girl, she'd wound up with a thirteen-year-old Paiute boy whom she was training to work on a drilling rig, which Zed was sure was against the rules. But then, rules meant zip to his sister. The boy, meanwhile, was teaching Jade Native American lore.

So his sister thought Karen Henderson was a nut case. He wasn't so sure. For some reason he was beginning to believe that Karen really did think he was Danny's father. But if her belief was based on nothing more tangible than that photo, she was grasping at straws. He hadn't gotten around to finding out more about the P.I., but after the test was over, that wouldn't be necessary.

Karen wasn't as striking as the redhead in the picture, her cousin Erin. From what he had seen of it under that red hat, Karen's hair seemed to be sort of a strawberry blond rather than a brilliant red. He could only wonder what her blue eyes might be like when they weren't shooting fire. Her wool shorts suit had shown off a good figure, neither top-heavy nor lacking, a build a man could appreciate. Furious as he'd been at her, he'd still noticed how cute she looked in those kneesocks. The truth was, if they hadn't been at loggerheads, he'd have been attracted to Karen.

Zed Adams was exactly how she'd imagined he'd be, Karen thought as she settled Danny into his crib at their Carson City motel. An arrogant, lying chauvinist. Erin, in her usual vague fashion, hadn't really told her anything about him, not even his name. "Gorgeously exotic," she'd said, dreamy eyed, as she dropped several photos into Karen's lap. "A fantastic lover."

Since Erin changed lovers as often as she changed the color of her nails, Karen hadn't thought to question her about the current one. Later, before Erin had taken off on a three-month cruise, Karen had asked if "he" was accompanying her. "Gone," Erin had said with a shrug. Either she hadn't yet realized she was pregnant or she'd chosen not to tell anyone.

Karen had never had another chance to ask her cousin about the man, Zed Adams.

Granted, he was good to look at, with a lethal combination of dark hair and eyes and well-delineated features. But "gorgeously exotic"? Not in those scruffy sweatpants that hung so dangerously low on his hips that she'd been distracted every time he moved, expecting disaster at any moment. Or was the right word anticipating? Hoping for?

She grimaced, disgusted with herself. Okay, so the creep was sexy. So what? She, for one, had no intention of sampling anything he had to offer.

Glancing at Danny, asleep on his stomach with his butt in the air, she made a silent vow. *We'll get him, kid. He'll pay for his despicable callousness.*

She checked her watch, noted it was after eight and picked up the phone book. Time to call around to find out where she could make an appointment for Zed to be tested. She hoped the technician who drew Zed's blood would use the dullest needle in creation. At least the DNA sampling wouldn't hurt Danny, or so she'd been told.

Before noon, pleased with her success, she left a message on Zed's answering machine, notifying him of the time and place of testing on the following day and telling him she'd meet him at the Reno clinic. "And you'd better show!" she warned before hanging up.

Rolling down his sleeve after the lab technician finished with him, Zed winced at the heartrending sobs seeping through the closed door of the next room. Damn it, that poor baby shouldn't have to go through this—and all for nothing. Zed wasn't the kid's father, as the tests would prove.

Karen had left the photo on his kitchen table. Jade had stopped by the ranch late yesterday afternoon and examined the picture carefully. "Hey, it's you, brother mine," she'd announced, "even to the cleft chin. No wonder this gal fingered you."

"But he's *not* me." A tinge of testiness had crept into his voice and Jade had caught it.

"You know I'm on your side. If you say you never met this redhead, I believe you." She'd taken another look at the photo. "Taken in San Diego, wasn't it? When were you last down there?"

"Let's see—I brought the sailboat up to Seattle two years ago and then to Tahoe the next year, where she still is. I haven't been to San Diego for at least two years, give or take a month or so."

"You say the baby's about six or seven months old?"

"I guess so. He can sit up by himself, anyway."

"Nine plus seven is sixteen months," she said. "So you couldn't have been in San Diego at the crucial moment when he was conceived. Of course, the fateful connection might not have taken place there."

"A lot of help you are."

"You don't need my help," she'd said, preparing to leave. "It wasn't you, as the blood tests will prove." At the door she'd paused and tossed a final remark over her shoulder. "Always providing the trickster's looking the other way."

"Trickster be damned," Zed muttered, not realizing he'd spoken aloud until he saw the lab technician eyeing him oddly. He shrugged and made his way back toward the waiting area.

Since they'd driven in separate cars, there was no reason to wait for Karen but he lingered, somehow reluctant to leave before she appeared with Danny. She'd dressed more casually this morning—a denim skirt with a shirt to match. He couldn't help but notice how the color set off her blue eyes, eyes that were wary today rather than angry.

Jade had insisted Danny was too young to be taught to say "Da" on cue, so he realized his suspicion—about Karen being responsible for what had sounded like an accusation yesterday—was unfounded. According to his sister, all babies said *da* and *ma* and *ba* without necessarily attaching any meaning to the sounds. Couldn't prove it by him, since—by choice—Danny was the first baby he'd been around for any length of time.

Which time had been too long. Remembering how he'd been forced to deal with the dirty diaper, Zed shook his head. Why the hell was he standing here waiting for the two of them when what he really wanted was for them to get out of his life as quickly as possible?

Karen emerged from the room where they'd drawn Danny's blood feeling as traumatized as he'd been. He'd stopped crying as soon as the technician finished, but he clung to her tenaciously, his head buried against her shoulder, an occasional whimper escaping.

"Poor baby," she murmured. "I'm sorry, but we had to do it to prove to that weasling—" She broke off as she noticed Zed's tall figure in the waiting room. Denying the sudden leap of her pulse, she frowned, asking herself why he was still here. Not out of the goodness of his heart, that was for sure.

"Is he okay?" Zed asked when she neared him.

Hearing his voice, Danny raised his head to look at Zed and offered him a tentative smile.

"Hello, Tiger," Zed said to him, surprising her with the warmth in his voice. "It was touch and go for a while there but I guess we both survived."

"Da," Danny said.

Zed looked at her. "That's yes in Russian, you know. Smart kid."

She didn't want to smile at him, but her lips curved up despite herself. "Yes, he is smart," she said.

"Hungry?" he asked as he opened the outer door for her.

She was, but she refused to admit it and shook her head.

"Too bad. John Ascuaga's Nugget has clam chowder to die for. I always stop by the Nugget's oyster bar when I'm in Reno. You get your choice of either white or red. Or both. Sure you don't want to change your mind?"

"We call those New England or Manhattan back East," she said, perfectly aware he must know this. "And no, I haven't changed my mind." She happened to love clam chowder but she wasn't about to tell him so, because she certainly wasn't going anywhere with him.

He slanted her a testy glance and drawled, "That's right, you did tell me you were a teacher. I sure hope I can remember which color belongs to which back East area."

Ignoring his understated sarcasm, she got right to the point. "I've asked them to send the test results to me. When I get them—"

"Wasn't that a tad high-handed?" he demanded. "Why not duplicate copies?"

She held on to her patience. "At this point we only need one report. When I have the results, I'll call you immediately."

"No way. No calls. I want to see the report in black and white. No fax or copies, either. On the original paper."

She tightened her lips. "All right, then, I'll bring them to your ranch. Then later, if you want your lawyer to have additional copies of—"

He held up a hand. "Stop right there. I won't need a lawyer because the test results will prove how mistaken you are. I don't know how this P.I. you hired ran me down, but he didn't find the right man, and neither did you. As I keep telling you, you're wasting your time. And your money."

"I think you have quite a surprise in store," she said, deliberately smiling because it seemed to annoy him.

"I agree that one of us will be surprised, all right, but it won't be me. How many times do I have to tell you I never met this cousin of yours? Furthermore, I've never donated sperm, so there is no possible way I can be Danny's father. Absolutely none."

"Da," Danny said, reaching a hand toward Zed, who was obviously taken aback.

Karen tried to stifle her laughter but failed. "I don't think he's speaking Russian this time," she said.

Chapter Two

Two days later Karen picked up the results of the blood tests at the Reno clinic.

The receptionist reminded her that the DNA test, which had to be sent away, would not be back for a week or so, adding, "At the earliest. We can't guarantee exactly when we'll receive it, so, since you don't live in Nevada, perhaps it'd be best if we asked them to send the DNA report to your California address."

Karen agreed. Checking over the blood test results, she smiled. The DNA test would be the clincher, but she couldn't help thinking that, actually, a DNA match would be the frosting on the cake.

While she was driving back to Carson City, rain began to spatter against her windshield, and when she reached Washoe Valley she found the wind had picked up. A sign that had been blank when she drove to Reno now was lit with a high-wind warning, prohibiting campers and trailers from traveling on U.S. 395 through the valley.

"Maybe I should have rented a midgrade car at the Frisco airport instead of this subcompact," she told Danny as she struggled against the gusts to keep the car in the lane.

Recalling that Mark Twain, during his stint in Virginia City, had labeled this wind "the Washoe zephyr," she smiled wryly. It was difficult to appreciate his sense of humor when the "zephyr" was doing its best to force her off the road.

The wind let up somewhat after she crested the hill and dropped down into Carson City, but by then the rain ran in rivulets across the hood of the car. Should she hole up in the motel or drive on into Carson Valley to Zed's ranch? Glancing at Danny, she saw he'd fallen asleep in his car seat. Darn. No matter where she stopped, he'd wake up. If she drove to the ranch he'd have a longer nap and might not be so cranky when he woke.

Besides, she was dying to shove the report under Zed's nose.

The rain thrumming against his windows prevented Zed from hearing the car pull up next to the house. Alerted by the slam of a car door, he strode into the living room, looked out and saw Karen, Danny in her arms, dashing through the rain. He opened the front door before she got there.

"I thought it never rained in Nevada," she complained as she entered.

He shrugged. "You're tuned in to the Nevada-is-awasteland-with-nothing-but-casinos syndrome like everyone else who doesn't live here.''

"I am not! I happen to think this area is beautiful. It's just that I didn't expect rain, so I'm not prepared."

Danny began to whimper.

"I'll get a towel so you can dry him off," Zed said.

"No need. Only his jacket is damp—he's dry enough underneath." Without being invited, she walked into the kitchen and, taking the same chair she'd used before, began to peel a layer of clothes off the boy. He struggled and fussed.

"Is there something wrong with him?" Zed asked.

"Not really. He was sleeping in the car on the way back from Reno and, when he naps, he tends to be cranky when he first wakes up."

"You can hardly blame him for that. So you've been to Reno." It wasn't a question. He knew she wouldn't be here unless she'd gotten the reports.

Karen glanced up at him. "Do sit down. You make me nervous hovering."

He was damned if he was going to ask her if she wanted anything. She'd refuse anyway. Sliding into a chair, he said, "Okay, I'm ready."

She pulled a cookie from a box labeled Arrowroot Biscuits. This was a biscuit, not a cookie? Could have fooled him. She shoved the cookie into Danny's hand—the left this time, he noted—flashed that false smile and said, "The DNA match won't be available for another week or so, but I did pick up the blood reports."

If he was reading her right, the blood match had turned out to be equivocal. Damn, he'd hoped to have this over without waiting for the DNA test. Saying nothing, he held out his hand.

Karen plunged her hand into her shoulder bag, pulled out an envelope and dropped it on the table in front of him. Extracting papers from the envelope, he saw that one was a report on Danny Henderson's blood and another on his. He looked at his first. Besides showing the type and Rh factor, there was an entire list of components he'd never heard of. He saw he was B negative, which he already knew, but what all the other letters and numbers meant was over his head.

He pulled Danny's report next to his. B negative. Even though her behavior had led him to suspect there might be a partial match, he was somewhat surprised that the boy also had this relatively rare blood type. He began going down the list of the other components, his eyes widening as he continued. *No,* he thought, *I don't believe this. She's pulling a scam.*

"The technician told me you have one very unusual blood component," Karen said. "Apparently it's quite rare. As you'll note, Danny has this same component. The two of you are, as she put it, a perfect match."

Which was completely impossible. Zed picked up Danny's report and waved it at her. "You faked this," he accused.

She glared at him. "How can you be so despicable? I might have known you'd try to weasel your way out of this. Isn't it bad enough that you deserted my pregnant cousin? Must you also deny the child you fathered?"

"I can't accept this report," he growled, ignoring her scathing remarks. "It's impossible!"

Karen took a deep breath and let it out slowly. "Go ahead—call the clinic if you don't believe me."

"You can be damn sure I will. I'm not the kid's father, and you're not going to pull a fast one."

"I'm not faking anything!" she cried. "I resent your accusation. But what else can I expect from a creep like you?"

"I'm not a creep!" he roared.

Danny burst into tears, burying his face in Karen's shoulder. "See what you've done?" she snapped. "Your shouting scared him."

"*My* shouting? What about yours?" Even as he spoke, Zed, wincing inwardly at the baby's sobbing, tried to grasp the ragged ends of his temper and bring it under control.

"Here," Karen said, thrusting the crying baby at him, a move that astonished him. "I need to get his things from the car and I refuse to take him out in the rain again."

Before he could come up with an alternative, Zed found himself holding Danny. Instinctively he cuddled the boy against him, patting his back. "It's all right, Tiger," he murmured. "Nobody's mad at you."

As he tried to soothe Danny, Zed was suddenly struck by what should have been clear from the beginning. The poor kid was not only fatherless, he was motherless. Erin was dead and God only knew who'd fathered him. It then occurred to Zed to wonder if Erin, who by Karen's account changed lovers often, had actually known who Danny's father was.

Unless the whole setup was a scam. He had only Karen's word that there *was* an Erin. But if it was a scam, why choose him? Money? The ranch was profitable but he was no millionaire, that was for sure.

Danny gave a heaving sob and twisted in his arms to look at him, ending his speculation.

"Hey, Tiger," Zed said softly. "I may not be your daddy, but you're safe with me."

Danny blinked teary eyes, then gazed around, obviously searching for Karen. At that moment she reentered the kitchen, water droplets clinging to her hair and bedewing her face. Despite his mistrust of her, Zed couldn't help but note how enchanting she looked. She set a large canvas bag on the table, brushed wetness from her shoulders and reached for Danny, who held out his arms to her.

"He's hungry," she said. "I need to feed him."

Zed surprised himself by saying, "I'll help if you'll tell me what to do."

She took him at his word, involving him in warming small jars of baby food and then a bottle of milk. He watched her feed Danny with a little spoon—a messy business that had him smiling at the way the kid managed to get as much food on her as in his mouth.

Come to think of it, *he* was hungry. Glancing at the clock, he saw it was nearly two. He'd missed lunch. No wonder. He'd be willing to bet Karen hadn't had anything to eat either.

If he asked her she'd probably refuse, so he wouldn't ask. "There's some of my sister's homemade lasagna in the freezer," he said. "I'll warm it up while you finish feeding little Tiger there." Without waiting for an answer he crossed to the refrigerator.

Karen opened her mouth to tell him not to bother, then closed it without speaking. She'd had nothing but an apple for breakfast and she was starved. Sharing lasagna with him didn't commit her to anything, and she really didn't want to leave until they settled what he planned to do about Danny. She hoped they could discuss the situation in a calm, rational manner. Maybe food would mellow him a trifle.

While he was fixing lunch, she finished feeding Danny and changed him. Apparently Zed noticed how he drooped against her shoulder, half-asleep, because he said, "Jade's old cradle is in one of the bedrooms, if you'd like to lay him down."

"Jade being your sister?" At his nod, she said, "Could you bring the cradle in here? Danny might be afraid in a strange room by himself."

Zed fetched the cradle. Danny settled into it as though it had been made for him and promptly fell asleep. She tucked his favorite stuffed toy, a blue horse, in beside him.

"Rather ratty, isn't it?" Zed commented. "The horse, I mean."

"He sucks on the ears," she said defensively. "I tried a pacifier but he wouldn't have anything to do with it. He wants the horse and throws a fit if he doesn't have it. The pediatrician said the material isn't toxic and I checked the ears—they're sewn on tight, so he won't choke."

"He's obviously strong-minded."

"You can say that again. But he's really sweet tempered if he gets his way." She half smiled. "Like a lot of males."

He acknowledged the gibe with raised eyebrows before removing a dish from the microwave. "Lunch is served," he told her. "Nothing but garlic bread and lasagna, but lots of both. What would you like to drink?"

"Hot tea, please, if you have it."

"Coming up."

For a long time they ate in silence, until Karen finally said, "Your sister makes delicious lasagna."

"I'll tell her you said so. She's going to be shocked about the blood match."

Karen eyed him warily. Did that comment mean he'd decided to take the reports at face value and drop his accusation about her falsifying them? "I take it you've discussed this with your sister," she said.

He nodded. "Jade and I don't have any other relatives, so we're pretty close." He set down his fork and gazed directly into her eyes. She was struck by how dark his were, a deep brown that seemed to verge into black.

"How old is Danny?" he asked.

"He was born May first," she said. "Several weeks premature."

"He's seven months old, then." Zed glanced over at the cradle. "The report says Danny Henderson, so evidently your cousin's name was the same as yours."

"Yes. Erin is—was—my father's brother's daughter."

"Did she tell you the man in that picture was Danny's father?"

Karen nodded.

"Did you always believe her?"

Not always, but she wasn't going to say so. Nor did she intend to repeat her unwise comment about Erin's many lovers. "In this case, I did believe her. Being pregnant made her so sick she wasn't interested in men. The pregnancy, in fact, led to her death, because she got eclampsia. That's a dangerous complication of pregnancy."

"So you were with her?"

Karen shook her head. "No. She went on this cruise and then remained down in the islands with an older woman she'd met on the ship. You see, Erin's grandmother left her a trust fund, so she could afford to indulge herself. Her mother is dead and she was more or less estranged from her father because he didn't approve of her life-style. She trusted me as much as she did anyone."

"When did you learn she was pregnant?"

Karen reminded herself that, as Danny's father, he had a right to have his questions answered, no matter whether she resented his asking or not. "Erin wrote me from the Virgin Islands shortly before she went into the hospital, sending me a legal form that made me the baby's guardian if anything happened to her. Naturally that alarmed me and I called her. By then she was in the hospital, on sedatives for the eclampsia, and I couldn't get her to make sense. I asked who the father was and she told me the man on the sailboat in the photos she'd given me."

"No name?"

"She either couldn't or wouldn't tell me. I flew to Bermuda a week later but it was too late—Erin was dead. The woman she'd been staying with had no idea who Danny's father was and had put 'unknown' on the birth certificate. I flew home to San Diego with Danny." Karen smiled slightly. "Believe me, I was scared to death at the thought of caring for a newborn baby."

"Okay," he said, sighing. "I may be playing the fool, but you've convinced me Erin existed and that Danny is her son. Not so much by the story you've told me—rather, I feel you're honest. Will you give me the benefit of the doubt about *my* honesty? Because, matching blood tests or not, there is no way I can be Danny's father.''

He'd almost lulled her into accepting him, but his last words brought her back to her senses. ''I suppose you're going to tell me you were out of the country at the time of conception.'' Sarcasm lent an edge to her voice.

Zed blinked. ''I'll be damned,'' he muttered after a moment or two of silence. ''It had to be a year ago in August, right? I wasn't exactly out of the country, but you're close. Last year Jade and I were in Alaska for the entire month of August.''

''Sure you were.''

''Jade will verify we were there.''

''And I'm supposed to believe your sister?''

''It's the truth, damn it!'' he bellowed. Almost immediately he turned to glance apprehensively at Danny, obviously worried that his raised voice might have disturbed Danny's sleep.

Disarmed by his show of concern—he did have a few redeeming qualities, after all—Karen abandoned her sarcasm. ''I have trouble believing you,'' she told him frankly. ''You've told me you and your sister are close, and relatives do tend to stick together. How can I accept her word as proof?''

''If you can't accept my word or hers, how about a videotape?'' His voice had dropped back to its normal range, she noted. ''We put one together in Alaska—or rather, Jade did—about well drilling in permafrost. I posed as a driller for the tape. The TV station in Anchorage aired our footage and interviewed both of us. I can't tell you the dates offhand, but Jade will have them. We visited Native American villages as well as the offshore islands and took innumerable pictures. As I recall, Jade also has a videotape of us salmon fishing.''

Karen bit her thumbnail as she digested this information. It did seem he'd actually been to Alaska with his sister during that crucial August. Not that there weren't daily flights between Alaska and California. Still, Erin had called her interlude with Danny's father an idyll, which implied a leisurely affair, not a fly-in-and-out one. Karen frowned, wondering why she'd thought of Erin's lover as Danny's father rather than Zed Adams. Because they were one and the same. Weren't they? For the first time a faint doubt crept into her mind and settled there.

He had to be Danny's father. Didn't the blood match prove it?

When she'd come back in with the baby bag she'd noticed how tenderly he was cuddling Danny. He might actually make a good father if he wasn't so stubborn about denying paternity. She loved Danny so much that she'd even be willing to help Zed raise him if no intimacy was involved. She definitely wanted no part of any involvement with Zed. With her cousin's lover.

But had he been? Despite the photos, somehow she couldn't imagine Erin and Zed together. Hey, she reminded herself, isn't Danny enough proof?

''If you like, I can call Jade and ask her to look up the dates and bring them to us, along with the videos and pictures,'' Zed said.

For a moment she couldn't grasp what he meant. Her thoughts had gone badly astray. Then she recalled they'd been speaking of the August dates when he claimed to have been in Alaska. ''Please do,'' she told him.

Zed pushed his empty plate aside and rose. As he

crossed to the phone, he glanced out the window and paused, noticing for the first time that the rain had turned to icy snow, rapidly accumulating atop the evergreen branches. He shook his head. The roads would be a mess. That skateboard Karen was driving would be all over the road. Ten to one she'd have an accident if she tried to drive back to Carson City.

Why hadn't he thought to check on the weather earlier? He could drive her, but in the ice and snow his pickup wouldn't be a hell of a lot safer than her skateboard. He hated to think of risking Danny's safety. In fact, he was damned if he meant to— even if Karen wasn't happy with his conclusions.

He reached for the phone and punched in Jade's number. "What's it like up there?" he asked when she answered. Jade lived on the mountain near Tahoe.

"Remember," she asked, "when we were kids and it snowed, how Grandma would tell us the angels were shaking the feathers out of their pillows? Well, it's king-size feather bed shake-out time up here at the moment. I'm staying in till it eases off."

"Don't blame you. Listen up." He told her about the blood match and what he needed from her. "Bring it down to me when you can, okay?"

"Will do," she said. "But that blood match bothers me. How could it have happened? Are you sure someone didn't make a mistake?"

"Anything's possible. Except that I'm the kid's father. No way."

"See you when I can make it," Jade told him, and hung up.

Zed turned to look at Karen, who was sipping her second cup of tea. She put down the cup when she caught his gaze. "Look out the window," he said.

She got up and did so. "Damn," she muttered.

"Exactly," he agreed. "I'm afraid you and Danny are stuck here for the night. It's too dangerous to try to make it into Carson City."

Her face took on the mulish look that he'd learned preceded an argument, then her expression changed and she sighed resignedly. "You're right. I can't take a chance, not with Danny. Why didn't you tell me it was going to snow?"

She could put his back up faster than any woman he'd ever met. "If I'd known, I certainly would have. They predicted rain on the morning report—no mention of ice or snow."

"I'm sorry, that was uncalled for," she said. "I can't blame you for the weather."

Much as she'd like to, he thought. But she *had* apologized.

"You provided lunch," she added. "Why don't you let me earn my keep by cooking the evening meal?"

Her proposal took him by surprise. "Sounds good to me," he said. Inspiration struck him. "I'll light a fire in the fireplace, make it nice and warm for Danny in there."

She reacted with enthusiasm. "Oh, good. If you have an old quilt or something like that, I'll put it on the floor so when he wakes up he can roll around and kick and hone his crawling skills. He's been pretty well confined to the car seat and the motel crib, and that's not good."

"We can eat by the fire if you'd like," he said. "To keep an eye on Tiger."

She nodded. "If you could show me what room Danny and I will be sleeping in, I'll move his stuff in there."

He led her down the hall and into the larger of the two guest bedrooms. There were actually four, but he used one for his office and the other wasn't completely furnished. "Jade stays over unexpectedly sometimes," he said, gesturing toward a dresser. "She keeps extra clothes in one of the drawers. Feel free to borrow whatever you need. She won't mind. She'll be down when the snow lets up."

"I hope that won't be too long," Karen said.

When Zed found himself wishing they were in for one of the Sierras' three-day storms, he shook his head. The sooner he got rid of Karen, the better.

After leaving her in the room, he began laying a fire, smiling to himself as he lit it. He might not be Danny's father and Karen sure as hell wasn't his wife, but it was almost as though the three of them were a family. The strange thing was he kind of liked the feeling.

As annoyed as she made him, he admired Karen's determination to find a father for Danny. Her devotion to the boy warmed his heart. He'd told himself earlier that the poor kid didn't have a mother, but the truth was Danny did. Karen was as loving a mother as if she'd borne him. Her tenderness when she'd laid him in the cradle had touched a part of him he hadn't realized existed.

The bottom line was another matter altogether. No man could be around Karen for long and not be seriously attracted to her. He'd seen her blue eyes stormy one moment, pensive the next. How would they look once her passion was aroused?

The fire caught, flaring up very much as he was beginning to do. Cool it, Adams, he told himself. So she was a cute blonde who'd fit into a man's arms just right, but if there ever was a woman who didn't want to be in *his* arms, Karen was the one.

Karen washed her hands and face in the bathroom off the bedroom. Finding the brush in her bag, she ran it through her hair, curlier than usual from the rain. Examining herself in the mirror, she decided she looked washed out. She'd brought lipstick with her but no other makeup. Not that it mattered, since she wasn't trying to impress Zed.

Although she no longer hated, loathed and detested him the way she had when she arrived, she certainly could never be interested in him, attractive as he was. When he gazed at her with those dark, dark eyes, she had difficulty keeping her mind focused on the matter at hand.

His consideration for Danny had surprised her—he actually seemed to like the boy, despite his refusal to admit he was the father. He didn't ignore him as so many men did. She smiled, remembering the nickname he'd bestowed on Danny. Tiger, he called him.

He hadn't tried to touch her. It hadn't even occurred accidentally. Maybe he didn't like her. Given the circumstances, she could understand why. What perplexed her was why it should bother her. *You don't expect every man you meet to find you attractive,* she chided herself, *and he's one man you don't want. You should be glad he pays more attention to Danny than he does to you.* But she wasn't.

Maybe the problem was she'd seen too much of him at their first meeting. Literally. He'd worn nothing but those about-to-fall-off sweatpants. All that well-put-together male flesh must have gotten to her core, which might explain why she was looking forward to this evening instead of resenting being forced to stay here.

When she came into the living room he was sitting on the couch in front of the fireplace staring into the flames licking at the logs. Before she realized what she meant to do, she eased down beside him. He glanced at her and smiled, the first genuine smile he'd given her.

"There's something about a fire," he said.

"Um," she agreed. "Cozy."

"Primitive," he said, his gaze holding hers. She felt herself falling into the dark pools of his eyes, where she might well drown. That wouldn't do. Making an intense effort, she looked away.

"Yes," she said in her best teacher voice. "Primitive man feared the darkness and knew fire was his friend and ally against the dangers of the night."

"Do you fear the night?" he asked, his voice low and soft.

"Sometimes," she admitted.

He moved his hand and she held her breath, waiting for his touch, wanting it. At that moment Danny made an inquiring sound from his cradle in the kitchen, his way of summoning her.

Karen jumped to her feet and the moment was over. But, she realized with mixed anticipation and apprehension, the evening was not over, much less the night.

Chapter Three

In Zed's fireplace lazy flames flickered between the glowing logs. On the floor, at a safe distance away from the fire, Danny lay on one of Grandma Adams's old quilts, amusing himself by getting up onto all fours and rocking back and forth. Almost as if he couldn't quite get his motor started, Zed thought with amusement.

He and Karen sat side by side on the couch to the left of the fireplace, sipping the remainder of the wine he'd found to serve with the tasty beef stew she'd cooked.

He couldn't recall feeling this content in a long time. Must be the result of a good meal and good wine because, as things stood, he sure as hell didn't have any reason to be content. Was he wrong to trust Karen? He glanced at her, no more than an arm's reach away from him, and found her looking at him, firelight mirrored in her eyes.

"I wish I could trust you," she said, and then blinked as though her own words had surprised her.

"Yeah," he said, "I know what you mean." He waved a hand to include the fire, the baby and the room in general. "This is great, but maybe it could be something more if we weren't at swords' points."

"It could?"

Turning to face her, he spoke softly. "Don't you think so?"

"I don't know. At the moment I'm not quite sure of anything. Must be the wine."

Danny moved an inch or so backward and crowed with triumph.

"Way to go, Tiger," Zed told him. "You'll be on your feet in no time." As he spoke, it occurred to him he wouldn't be around to see the boy take his first step. Why that should matter he hadn't a clue, but oddly enough, it did.

What *was* going to happen to Danny? Would Karen ever find his real father? And, if she did, would the man acknowledge his son? Would he treat him with love and tenderness?

"Yeah," he said, referring to his own thoughts, "it must be the wine."

"If I trust you," Karen said hesitantly, "I'll have to believe you never met my cousin. And if that's true, then who *is* the man with Erin on that sailboat? And why does he look exactly like you?"

"Beats me. I heard somewhere that we all have a double somewhere on this earth, but I didn't believe it. I'll admit he's a dead ringer for me—can't blame you for having doubts."

"You're really not Danny's father?" she asked.

"Not a chance."

"Then you weren't Erin's lover, either."

"You got it," he agreed. "No lover, no baby."

"You really aren't her type."

Zed raised his eyebrows.

Karen looked away from him. "I mean, she preferred flashy types. You know, fast sports cars and things like that."

"I drive a pickup—I suppose that labels me as stodgy. Thanks a lot."

"I didn't mean you weren't attractive." Embarrassment tinged her words. "Actually, you are. Good Lord, what am I saying?" Her hands rose to her cheeks as though trying to hide her flush.

Zed leaned to her and gently removed her hands from her face, taking them in his own. "That's the nicest thing you've said to me since we met," he murmured. "Now it's my turn. We stodgy but attractive types happen to prefer blue-eyed strawberry blondes, not fiery redheads. Especially when we meet one as pretty as you."

He knew better than to kiss her, but gazing into her blue eyes seemed to throw his brain out of gear. Her lips, slightly parted, were close to his and her scent, floral and woman, doubly enticing, surrounded him, obliterating any reservations he had left. Releasing her hands, he pulled her into his arms and slanted his mouth over hers.

The feel of her lips, soft and warm and responsive under his, was unexpectedly potent, making him realize one kiss wasn't going to be enough, not by a long shot. If this was a mistake, it was going to be a double jackpot one— and he didn't give a damn.

Karen didn't resist being drawn into his embrace—how could she when he'd already mesmerized her with his dark gaze? One kiss, she thought bemusedly. What harm is there in one kiss? Then his mouth covered hers and the blaze his lips kindled inside her rivaled the flames in the fireplace. Her arms tightened around him, holding him to her as she savored his taste, more potent than the wine she'd already had.

If this was a mistake, as some small part of her insisted, then it was a mistake she enjoyed making, one she wanted to make. If there were any regrets, she would deal with them later.

She was vaguely conscious of Danny's contented babbling. The sounds seemed an appropriate accompaniment to what was happening, though contentment didn't begin to describe what Zed's caresses evoked in her.

Dangerous. What she was feeling, what she was doing, what she was letting him do was dangerous. But, oh, so delicious. How could she stop?

She slid her hands under his T-shirt, caressing his back, feeling the erotic smoothness of his skin and the flex of the powerful muscles underneath as he shifted position so that they were lying on the couch, his arousal hard against her.

Whoa, I can't do this! she thought, even though she was as aroused as he was. We can't. What are we thinking of?

They weren't thinking; that was the trouble.

"Zed," she gasped, trying to struggle free. "Stop!"

For a moment his arms tightened around her and then he let her go. She slid away from him and stumbled to her feet, trying to pull down her shirt and run a hand through her disordered hair at the same time.

Zed sat up slowly. She didn't want to meet his gaze, but couldn't help doing so. He smiled at her ruefully. No man had ever looked so sexy to her.

"Got a tad carried away, didn't we?" His voice, roughened by passion, sent a shiver along her spine.

Caught again by his dark gaze, she couldn't seem to catch her breath. She still wanted to touch him, to have him touch her, to be in his arms....

"Da!" Danny exclaimed loudly. "Da, da!"

The tension between them evaporated, changing to laughter.

"He always has the last word," Zed observed. "And it's always the same one."

After that, the evening was anticlimactic. The fire gradually died down and Danny grew sleepy, so Zed moved the cradle back into the bedroom.

"I'll go to bed with him," she said.

Zed's look clearly told her that he wished she'd chosen him instead.

"What I mean," she added hastily, "is that he might be frightened in a strange place if I'm not in the same room with him."

When they said good-night he made no attempt to kiss her—a wise move, although disappointment mingled with her relief. Danny fell asleep in the cradle even before she undressed. She put on a sleep-T she found among Jade's things and slid into bed, where she tossed and turned, her mind roiling with unanswered questions.

After what had happened between them tonight, she couldn't revert to believing Zed was lying to her. And yet, if the man in the photo wasn't him, who could it be? The P.I. she'd hired had tried to identify him by showing the photo to the people who handled the slip permits at the San Diego Bay marina.

He'd had no luck until he ran into a woman who'd worked there up until last year but was now employed elsewhere. She'd been visiting a friend at the marina, had seen the photo and had identified "the dreamboat with fantastic buns" as Zed Adams. He *was* memorable, no doubt about that. God knows she'd never forget him.

Anyway, from what he called his sources—she didn't know what those were—the P.I. had eventually discovered where Zed lived, checked him out and told her he had a match. After she'd seen the pictures he'd surreptitiously taken of Zed Adams, she, like the P.I., had been sure they'd hit on the right man.

Now she wasn't sure at all. Not that she ruled him out completely. And, until she did, there would be no more fooling around. A smile curved her lips as she remembered him calling himself stodgy. If tonight was any example, he was as far from stodgy as wrong was from right.

Karen sighed and turned over in bed one more time. If only she knew what was wrong and what was right. What was the truth?

Zed couldn't sleep. Not with Karen in bed just down the hall from him. He hadn't yet seen her naked, so he pictured her wearing that long T-shirt Jade used for nightwear. Come to think of it, she and his sister were about the same size, which made her around five-three and about 110 pounds. He'd never in his life thought of Jade as sexy, but Karen certainly was.

And here she was within his reach, wearing nothing but the T-shirt. If she'd had that on when they were in the living room... He shook his head. He was never going to get to sleep this way.

He had no intention of going down the hall. Unless she invited him, he'd stay out of her bed. Even if she did invite him, he'd be smart not to get any more involved with Karen than he already was. Because of Erin and Danny and that damn blood match, she represented nothing but trouble. But never had trouble looked so enticing.

Despite falling asleep late, he woke early to an unfamiliar sound. Confused for a moment, he sat up and listened. A baby was crying. Danny. Zed rolled out of bed and started down the hall just as Karen, fully dressed, opened her bedroom door with Danny in her arms. She stared at Zed, her eyes widening.

"Oh!" she exclaimed.

At that point he remembered he was naked, and made a mad dash to grab a pair of sweatpants.

"Sorry," he muttered when he came into the kitchen. "I forgot. Need help with Tiger?"

Moments later he found himself warming little jars of baby food again, a task that seemed almost pleasantly familiar.

As he carried the jars to the table, Karen said, "They're going to fall off."

"What—the jars?"

"Your pants. They're barely hanging on your hips."

"They've never fallen off yet," he grumbled as he yanked them up around his waist, only to feel them slide down again.

"You might try tying them tighter," she said.

Let a woman into your life even a tad and she tries to change you, he thought. Padding over to get a cup of coffee, he discovered he'd forgotten to put new grounds in and turn on the programmer. "Damn," he muttered as he corrected his oversight.

"Grouchy without your caffeine?" she asked.

"Don't tell me you drink decaf?"

She nodded smugly.

"May the good Lord protect me from caffeine-free women," he said. "You're as bad as my sister."

"It's stopped snowing," she said.

"I noticed, but the plow hasn't been by yet. The ranch feed-in road isn't a main one and I'm not a buddy of the current politicos, so it takes them a while to get around to me. You're stuck here until the plow does show."

"I guess I can live with that."

"My turn to cook," he said. "French toast okay?"

"As my mother always said, 'The cook calls the shots.'"

"Is she still alive?" he asked. "Your mother, I mean."

Karen thought it an odd question but harmless enough. "Yes. She and my dad live in upstate New York. I've tried for years to get them to move to San Diego, but they like it where they are, cold weather and all." As she finished, she remembered him saying that he and his sister were the only two left in his family. Was that the reason he'd asked the question?

"What do they think of you being left with Danny?" he said.

The boy turned to look at Zed and grinned at him, cereal drooling down his chin. Karen caught the runover with the spoon and tried to interest him in taking another mouthful, but Danny turned away from the spoon, reaching his arms out to Zed.

"Hey, Tiger," Zed said, and plucked him from her lap, ignoring the cereal-smeared bib as well as Danny's messy face. "Want to help me make French toast?"

If he didn't mind cereal splotches on his bare chest, she wasn't about to protest. What he'd asked her was another matter. "I don't think I can answer your question without giving you some family background," she said.

"Fire away."

"Dad's brother lived in the same small New York town as we did, so Erin and I were more or less raised together until they moved away when she was thirteen. We always kept in touch. After I finished college I took a teaching job in San Diego and liked it there, so I stayed. Erin, who'd been living in Manhattan, followed me out to California and bought a condo. By this time her mother was dead and her father had remarried. His new wife and Erin didn't get along. Actually, her father had sort of given up on Erin before that. My parents hadn't, though. They were pleased when she moved to San Diego because they believed I could keep an eye on her and curtail what they called her 'wildness.'"

Karen shook her head. "Erin did her thing no matter what anyone thought or said. Even when she asked for advice, she didn't take it. She was fun and I loved her, but she was a first-class, gold-medal risk taker. She thrived on danger."

Zed, Danny in the crook of one arm, turned from the refrigerator, two eggs in his other hand. "I take it you're the look-before-you-leap type."

She half smiled. "Just call me Ms. Stodgy."

He chuckled. "No way, not unless you own a pickup. So you were elected to run herd on your maverick cousin, and you found it a hopeless task."

Caught up in her memories of Erin, Karen got up and skirted the counter to be closer to Zed, as if that would make it easier to explain how she'd felt. "We might not have seen eye-to-eye but we were friends. She was always the one who got into impossible situations and needed my help to extricate herself, but I knew if I ever was in trouble she'd do the same for me."

"Now I understand why you wound up with Danny."

Karen sighed. "My parents don't actually disapprove, but I get the feeling they think Erin stuck me with what should have been her problem." She wasn't going to tell him that her mother had told her in no uncertain terms that her chances of marriage were much poorer now that she was burdened with Danny.

"Even if he isn't yours by birth," her mother had added, "a prospective husband doesn't like to raise another man's child. It's human nature."

A low rumble coming from outside caught her attention and sent her to the window, but she couldn't see the road. "The plow?" she asked Zed.

"Sounds like it."

She had no more excuse to stay. Fighting her reluctance to leave, she said, "I'd better get Danny's stuff together. Do you want me to take him?"

Zed shook his head. "Tiger's doing fine where he is."

He watched Karen leave the kitchen, admiring the way her jeans clung to her rounded butt, and remembered how good she'd felt next to him last night on the couch.

"Whoa, Tiger," he muttered, "old Zed better keep his mind on what he's doing instead of what he'd like to do."

The roar of dual pipes alerted him to the fact that Jade was arriving, her four-wheel negotiating his unplowed drive. His impatient sister must have trailed the county plow to get here. She parked in front rather than risking the pile of snow at the kitchen door.

Carrying Danny, he padded to the front door, opening it as Jade was stomping the snow from her boots on the stoop.

"Good grief!" she exclaimed as she entered. "I didn't expect you to take to fatherhood so quickly. What a pair of messy males! At least he's got more clothes on than you have."

She smiled at Danny, saying, "Hi, honey."

Zed watched him examine her solemnly, exactly as the boy had done to him at the first meeting.

"You didn't tell me his eyes were green, like mine and our mother's," Jade accused. "He's kind of light haired to be yours, though."

"You know perfectly well I'm not his father."

Jade tipped her head to the side, strands of her long chestnut hair falling across her face. She pushed it back and assessed Danny. "He's got an incipient cleft in his chin," she noted. "It'll probably deepen as he gets older. Like yours did."

"Don't forget the guy in the photo also has a cleft chin," he reminded her, aware she was teasing him and trying not to get uptight, even though he didn't consider this a joking matter.

"Oh, *that* guy," she said, sliding off her jacket. "I smell coffee—hope it's decaf."

"Nope. I've got that instant stuff you left here so you can heat water for your lily-livered brew in the microwave. Make it two cups—Karen drinks decaf, too."

"Da!" Danny exclaimed, patting Zed's face as they walked into the kitchen.

Jade looked startled. "Is he talking to you?"

"Not really. He only speaks Russian."

"I hope you realize you're both covered with glueylooking crud."

Zed shrugged. "It's baby cereal. Nothing a shower won't cure."

"You shower with that baby?" Jade asked.

"You must be Jade," Karen said. Neither of them had heard her come into the kitchen, and they both turned to look at her. Danny leaned toward her, holding out his arms, and Zed relinquished him.

"You're obviously Karen." Jade's voice, while not markedly cool, lacked warmth.

"I hope you don't mind that I used your sleep-T last night," Karen said. "I wasn't expecting to get snowed in."

Jade glanced from Karen to Zed and back to Karen. After a marked silence, she said, "So what's for breakfast? I'm starved."

"Zed was making French toast. But now that the plow's been through I really ought to get going."

"Please don't leave," Jade said. "I've brought some photos and two videocassettes I think you'll be interested in seeing. I'll take over the French toast while my brother showers and puts on a few more clothes. Then we'll eat and take a look at the pictures."

Zed went off without protest and Karen decided she

should stay, since she really did need to see Jade's so-called proof. Jade was certainly an organizer, she thought as she removed Danny's bib and wiped his smeared face and hands with a wet cloth.

"Do you have a ranch, too?" she asked, curious to know what Jade did for a living.

Jade shook her head without turning from the stove. "I run the drilling company," she said.

"Drilling company?" Karen echoed. "Oh, that's right, Zed said that you videotaped drilling in Alaska. I had no idea you ran a drilling company, though."

"I'm a groundwater geologist. We inherited the company when our grandparents died. Zed always wanted to live on the land, so he took the ranch and I took the company. Grandpa never could get it through his head that women are as capable as men in any field, so Zed, being male, had to work with him while our grandfather was alive. Grandpa often said I should have been a boy, because I had a natural talent for well drilling. Water, that is. We don't do oil."

Since Jade was approximately the same size she was—small—Karen couldn't picture her as a well driller. "I always thought drilling must take a lot of brute strength," she said.

Jade turned to look at her. "I know the ropes, so I tell the brutes how to do it. Usually, anyway. I've found that anything's possible in my field and I have been known to get down and dirty with the best of them. I understand you're a teacher. A nice, clean job that, as I see it, can drive you right up the wall on a daily basis."

Karen smiled, liking Jade better every minute. "You got it. I live on that wall."

Jade returned her smile, but briefly. Waving her spatula for emphasis, she said, "My brother has his flaws, like all males, but he's not a liar. I saw your photo and I agree that man could be Zed's clone but, apart from the fact he was with me in Alaska during the crucial implantation time, if he says he isn't Danny's father, then he isn't."

"I didn't believe him at first," Karen admitted. "After all, the private detective I'd hired had tracked him down using the photo and, as you say, there's such a close resemblance to the man in the photo. Then there's the blood match, which is hard to explain if he's not Danny's father. I've been wondering—why did your grandparents raise the two of you?"

Jade turned back to the stove, leading Karen to believe she might not answer. "I don't mean to pry," she added.

"You're not," Jade said. "I was just trying to organize my explanation. Our mother died when I was born—Zed was almost four at the time. We lived in Los Angeles then but moved here to Nevada while I was still a baby. Our father—" She paused before going on. "We never knew him. He had died before I was born—we were told when we were old enough to ask. That was why our mother had come home to live with them. Our grandparents seemed reluctant to talk about him, saying they knew very little. Grandma once let it slip that my mother had married him against their wishes."

"No aunts or uncles or cousins?"

"None. Just the two of us."

"Danny slept in your cradle last night," Karen said, abandoning the questioning that hadn't led anywhere and not wanting to return to why she had a problem with believing Zed.

Jade turned to her again. "That cradle is the only thing we have that came from our father's side of the family. He was supposed to have slept in it when he was a boy. I don't know why Zed refers to the cradle as mine—he must have slept in it, too, when he was a baby." She cocked her head assessingly, brushing back a lock of hair that fell over her eye. "You've changed your mind about Zed since you've been here, haven't you? I mean despite the photo and the blood match."

Karen hesitated, then nodded. "You're right, actually, I have—with reservations."

"Reservations?" Zed's voice said from behind her. "About what?"

Unwilling to discuss how she felt with Zed, Karen thought quickly. "For my trip back to San Diego," she said. "My flight leaves from Frisco two days from now."

"Why did you fly into San Francisco?" Jade asked.

Karen shrugged. "I realize now that Reno would have been a better choice, but at the time I didn't know."

"You thought everything would be settled in a week's time?" Zed demanded.

"I'm a teacher," she reminded him. "I could only afford to take off a week."

"The French toast is ready," Jade said. "Someone better set the table."

While eating they discussed the weather and what her chances of getting over the Sierras in what Zed kept referring to as a skateboard would be if it snowed again. Not good was the consensus.

"The best solution is for me to go along with you," he said finally. "I've been over those mountains in every kind of weather."

Karen would have liked to insist that she was perfectly capable of driving alone no matter what the weather, but the problem was she wouldn't be alone—Danny would be with her. With him along, she wasn't willing to take the risk of being stranded. "You'd fly back to Reno from Frisco?" she asked, postponing her final agreement.

He raised his eyebrows. "No. I'm going all the way to San Diego with you."

"That's not necessary," she snapped.

"But it is," he insisted. "Danny has a father somewhere. What better place to search for him than in the place where the picture was taken?"

Karen stared at him, speechless, momentarily taking her attention away from Danny, who immediately plunged his hands into the remains of her maple-syrup-covered French toast and then shoved his sticky fingers into his mouth, obviously enjoying the sweet taste.

"See?" Zed said. "You've got your hands full with Tiger and teaching besides. This is a slow season for ranching—my foreman can take care of what little has to be done—so I'm free to spend my time searching. I also have the advantage of looking like the man I'm searching for."

Karen couldn't deny she could use his help. What troubled her was having him so close at hand—in the same city with her. They'd obviously get together often to discuss his search. Would she have enough sense—or should she say willpower?—to keep from falling into his arms at the first opportunity?

"I don't know..." she began.

"I do," he said. "Right, Jade?"

"Sounds good to me," Jade responded. "I've got one

well to finish up and then I'll have some slack time, too. Want my help?''

"Why not?" Zed asked. "You've always been more devious than me, and that might be useful.''

Jade snorted.

"How about you, Tiger?" Zed asked, reaching over to ruffle Danny's hair. "What's your opinion?"

Danny grabbed Zed's hand with his sticky fingers and then opened his mouth. Karen sighed in resignation as she waited for the inevitable.

"Da," Danny said enthusiastically as he tried to taste Zed's middle finger. "Da, da."

Jade glanced from Karen to Zed. "Russian, my eye,'' she said. "A likely excuse. The kid's calling you Daddy.''

Chapter Four

As they deplaned from the jet at Lindbergh Field in San Diego, Karen finally blurted out what she'd been trying to find a tactful way to say from the beginning of their trip south. "I live in a very small one-bedroom apartment. There's hardly even room for Danny, so I can't invite you to stay with us."

Shifting the sleeping boy to his other arm, Zed said, "I wasn't expecting you to put me up. I'll find a bayside motel tonight. After that I hope to rent a sailboat for the time I'm here, and I'll sleep on the boat. That seems the logical way to begin the search, since I haven't a clue except for the *Maddamti*."

Karen had stared at that odd name often enough in her many examinations of the photo of Erin and Danny's father, and had wondered what it meant, if anything. "Does the name of that sailboat mean anything to you?'' she asked.

He shook his head. ''Sailors often make up strange names to call their boats—it's a very personal thing, akin to naming a child. We may never find out what *Maddamti* means.''

''The private detective did discover no boat by that name was currently docked here,'' she said. ''He also learned they register the boats by their number and, since that wasn't visible in the photo, he had no way to trace the owner. It didn't occur to me before to research the name, but it's worth a try, don't you think? I know one of the reference librarians at the downtown library—I'll call her and ask her to check and see if it's a foreign word of some kind.''

''Good idea. We need all the help we can get.''

Karen marveled at how she had made almost a complete turnaround in her beliefs since she'd met Zed. From being convinced he was the man who'd fathered Erin's child, she'd come to accept that he probably wasn't. It was mind-boggling to realize he was here in San Diego helping with her search for the man in the photo. If that man really wasn't Zed. A niggling doubt still remained despite viewing Jade's convincing Alaskan videos.

Later, after ransoming her car from the airport parking lot and dropping Zed at a motel, Karen drove east along the freeway toward her La Mesa apartment. Her mind wasn't on Danny or the search but rather was filled with remembering the devastating feel of Zed's lips on hers and the sensual warmth of being in his arms. She didn't dare succumb to her longing to have him hold her again. How could she want him to kiss her when she wasn't completely convinced he was being honest with her? Unfortunately, that fact didn't diminish her attraction to him.

"I'll have to watch myself as much as I do him," she told the sleeping Danny. Easy to say, hard to do, but somehow she'd manage. She had to.

The next morning Zed walked along the waterfront, pausing when he reached the *Star of India* to admire the 1863 bark, the oldest merchantman afloat. Amazing how seaworthy she still was. Those Isle of Man shipwrights certainly knew their craft. After years and years of neglect, she'd been restorable. Even with her sails furled she was a magnificent sight. If you loved ships, as he did, the *Star* was almost alive.

Alive or not, unfortunately she couldn't tell him who the hell the man aboard the *Maddamti* had been. His job was to find someone who could. Not only to get himself out from under but to provide Danny with a father and, not so incidentally, to relieve Karen of the burden of trying to raise the boy alone.

Zed strolled on, savoring the mild, damp morning, the Southern California coast weather so different from Nevada. He wouldn't change where he lived for any amount of money, but he did love the sea. The sight of the sailboats moored in the marina made him long to be out on the ocean flying before the wind.

He smiled as a thought struck him. Sailing was his joy and his passion. He sailed wearing only shorts but he'd never sailed naked—what would it be like? Awesome, he was sure. If he didn't freeze his buns off.

Once at the marina, he surveyed the boats, choosing several he'd be interested in renting temporarily if their owners would agree. He jotted down sailboat names and numbers, then checked his watch. Karen would be up by now; she might even be off to school already. He'd resisted the urge to call her earlier, telling himself not to play the fool, to wait and call when he had something positive to report.

Staring at the boats without really seeing them, he thought about his few days with Karen. He hadn't dreamed it was possible to miss anyone so much after so short an acquaintance. He actually missed Tiger, too, and wondered how long the kid would remember him. How much did seven-month-old babies remember? He didn't have a clue.

A man's voice jarred him from his reverie. "Admiring my boat? She's a nice one, ain't she? Wish I could take her out oftener."

Zed turned to see a sixtyish man wearing casual clothes topped by a yachting cap. He was leaning on a horse-headed cane.

"She's a beaut," Zed agreed. "Actually, I was wondering if I could rent her for a week or so. My sailboat's moored up at Lake Tahoe at the moment. I'm here for several weeks and it's hard to be in San Diego without sails."

The man examined him carefully. "Never occurred to me to rent her," he said slowly. "Not sure I want to. Be willing to show you around her, though."

"That's kind of you." Zed offered his hand. "My name's Zed Adams. I'm a rancher from Nevada, near Carson City."

"George Stone," the man said as they shook hands. "My old daddy, God rest his soul, was a Texas rancher, worked his butt off. Mine, too, when I was a kid. Got out of there as soon as I could."

Zed grinned. "I know what you mean about work, but I happen to like ranching."

George raised his eyebrows. "Takes all kinds."

The *Painted Lady* had been meticulously cared for, Zed observed when he went aboard. After her owner had given him the grand tour of the boat and he'd honestly admired her qualities, he said, "I understand why you're reluctant to rent her. This is the most shipshape rig I've ever been on."

George turned from him and looked out over the water, one hand covering his mouth. "Tell you what," he said finally, swiveling to face Zed. "I know a real sailor when I meet one. Give me some information so I can check you out, and the phone number where you're staying. Ain't promising anything, mind you, but might be we can make a deal, after all."

After George left, Zed wandered around the marina, striking up conversations when he could and mentioning the *Maddamti*. No one he talked to had ever heard the name or seen the boat. Asking about a man who looked like him proved equally fruitless. Eventually, a feeling he hadn't had since he was a child began to creep over him— the sensation that something was missing, something unknown. He'd hated the feeling then and he didn't care for it now. Hoping to rid himself of the unpleasant sensation, he called his sister, by some miracle catching her at the drilling office.

"Just checking in," he said. "Thought I'd leave the motel number."

"Okay," Jade told him, "but Karen gave me hers, you

know, so I can always find you if I have to. Speaking of Karen, I didn't get the chance to ask you what's going on between the two of you.''

"Nothing," he said firmly.

"Come on, brother mine, I've been a big girl for quite a few years now. The two of you are obviously on the verge of—"

"Of nothing. With this paternity business she's dangling over my head, Karen's the last woman I intend to get involved with."

"Okay, I'll grant that your intentions are good. But Grandma always told me the road to hell was paved with good intentions. At the ranch the air was positively sizzling with the electricity you two were generating."

"All right—she's pretty, I'm attracted. So what? I'm not going to act on any crazy impulse."

"You turn her on, too. That's a dangerous combination."

"You hit on the right word," he admitted. "Dangerous. I know trouble when I see it. I'd be a damn fool to plunge headlong into an affair with her. I'm here because I need to find the man in that photo to clear myself and, in the process, to give Danny a father."

Jade sighed. "He deserves someone better than a jerk who'd run out on a pregnant woman."

"I'm beginning to wonder if the guy ever knew. Erin sounds like she was enough of an airhead not to realize what was happening to her until after the guy split."

"She'd know." Jade's tone allowed no room for argument. "Also, she must have had some idea of how to get in touch with him."

"If I can't locate him, we'll never find out whether he knew about Erin's pregnancy or not."

"Hang in there. It's only been one day. I'll be down sometime next week with a six-pack of deviousness stuffed in my backpack."

Zed grinned, feeling better, his strange mood dissipating. "I'll keep in touch," he said, and hung up.

After lunch he returned to his motel room and, since Karen had offered to sign a release-of-information form, he called the private eye's office and made an appointment to talk to him the following afternoon. No point in going over ground the guy might already have covered.

Fighting a return of his earlier strange mood, he decided to get out of the room, and was about to leave when the phone rang.

"Oh, good," Karen said when he answered. "I hoped I might catch you in. I couldn't wait until this evening to tell you what I found out, so I'm calling on my break. I didn't have to phone the reference librarian. This morning in the teacher's lounge I mentioned that I was trying to find out what *Maddamti* meant. One of the women is married to an Arab and is taking a course in his language. Our mysterious word happens to be one she's already learned. *Maddamti* means 'my lady' in Arabic."

"In Arabic?" Zed echoed, frowning.

"Yes. Maybe that'll give us something to go on, don't you think?"

She sounded so upbeat that he conjured up an enthusiasm he didn't really feel. "Great. I'll see what I can do with the info." He found he didn't want to end the conversation. "Danny okay?" he asked.

"Yes, but I guess he's been with me too much the past

week, because he cried when I left him with the baby-sitter this morning. Ordinarily he's happy with her.''

"Maybe he misses me." Zed was only half joking.

A short silence ensued. "He hardly knows you," she said finally.

Zed decided he couldn't feel much worse than he already did, so he might as well go for broke. "I'd like to come over and see both of you this evening," he said. "Sort of touch base. I'll bring pizza or Mexican or Chinese. Take your pick."

Karen, grimacing in disgust at the way her pulse sped up, told herself she'd simply thank him but add that she was busy. Instead, she said, "Pizza sounds good. But no wine!"

He chuckled.

"Do you know how to get to my place?" she asked.

"I have the address, I have a map and I'll be renting a car. See you later."

That evening, while Karen was rushing around trying to make the apartment half-presentable, she came across one of her copies of the photo of Erin and Danny's father. Pausing, she examined the man critically. Dark hair and eyes and tanned skin didn't necessarily add up to him being Arabic, but it didn't prove he wasn't, either.

She thought of her cousin saying, "Gone," when she'd asked if the man was accompanying Erin on the cruise. Was it possible her cousin had meant he'd left the States to return to his own country? That could be the reason Erin was never able to locate him—if she'd tried. Karen shook her head. All this was nothing but speculation based on the boat's Arabic name.

The doorbell rang. She dropped the photo, took a quick

glance around and hurried to the door. Peering through the spy-eye confirmed it was Zed and she let him in. "If he's gone back to the Middle East," she said in lieu of a greeting, "we'll never find him."

Zed handed her the pizza box he carried and said, "Who won't we find?"

Before she could explain her reasoning, Danny, who had been playing contentedly in his playpen in the living room, began to babble excitedly. Zed looked at him, smiled and said, "Hey, Tiger, what's up?" Setting down a pack of soft drinks, he crossed to the playpen, leaned over and lifted the boy into his arms.

Danny grinned happily and patted Zed's face.

"See," Zed said, "he *did* miss me."

Karen couldn't argue—it was obvious Danny remembered Zed and was delighted by his presence. To tell the truth, she was equally pleased to see him. Not that she meant to be as demonstrative as Danny about it. Or even say so.

"I constructed a scenario about Erin's lover being Arabic," she told Zed. "If he has left the States the search may be hopeless."

Zed shrugged. "If he is an Arab, he could just as well live in this country. Anyway, he looks like me and I've never been taken for an Arab—though I'm occasionally pegged as a Native American."

"But *Maddamti?*"

"Boat owners choose names for all sorts of reasons and in all kinds of languages. I'll admit I haven't run across an Arabic name before, but I don't really consider it unusual. There's probably some tie-in, if we can figure out what it might be."

"Over dinner," she said, retreating to the kitchen with the pizza. Glancing over her shoulder, she saw Zed pick up the soft drink pack he'd brought and follow her.

While she set out the salad she'd prepared, he sat on a chair, Danny on his knee, and jiggled him up and down while the boy shrieked with glee.

When she sat down to eat, she tried to take Danny and put him in his high chair, but he scowled at her and clung to Zed. "He's okay with me," Zed told her.

"You don't have any idea what you're letting yourself in for," she said. "I hope you can keep him out of your pizza. Better give him one of his cookies." She gestured toward a small plate in the middle of the table. "I warn you—what's within his reach, he tends to grab."

Zed managed with surprising dexterity for someone who wasn't accustomed to handling babies, she thought. He fended off Danny's attempts to intercept what went into his mouth and kept baby fingers out of his plate. Not until they were almost finished did he make the fatal error of leaving his soft drink within the boy's range. Danny lunged toward the glass, hands extended, and over it went. Toward Zed, naturally, so that the fizzy liquid drained into his lap.

"Whoa, Tiger!" Zed exclaimed, too late. He handed the boy to her and began mopping up.

Karen placed Danny in the high chair, dropping several of his favorite toys on the tray before coming to Zed's assistance.

Danny promptly threw the toys on the floor, into the sticky mess Zed was trying to wipe up. "Da!" he said imperiously.

"If you think I'm going to pick up your toys after you

dumped soda all over me and the floor you're badly mistaken,'' Zed told him. He shoved them under the high chair.

In an effort to see where the toys had gone Danny leaned so far over the side of the chair that Karen, fearing he'd topple over, took him out and plopped him into the playpen. That didn't suit him at all and he complained loudly.

"Tiger sounds a tad annoyed," Zed remarked.

"And a touch spoiled, too, I'm afraid," she said ruefully.

It wasn't until later, after she'd put Danny to bed, that she and Zed had a chance to talk. "Thank heaven he's always been a sound sleeper," she said, easing down onto the chair next to the couch, where Zed was. "I've heard horror stories from some of the teachers I work with about babies his age still waking every two hours during the night and demanding attention."

"I'm no expert on babies, but I wouldn't put up with that situation very long," Zed said. "I don't think you would, either—and Tiger probably senses it. He's one smart kid. Which reminds me—tomorrow's Friday. What do you have planned for you and the boy this weekend?"

Words leapt to her lips unbidden. "I thought we'd help you."

"Good. A couple with a baby is less intimidating to people than a man alone. We'll cruise the marina with the photo and talk to anyone who doesn't growl at us. I'll be meeting with your P.I. tomorrow—maybe he'll come up with a new angle."

"You don't think the man—Danny's father—could be Arabic?" she asked.

"If he was, wouldn't Erin have told you?"

Karen thought about it. "Maybe. But not necessarily. In many ways she was secretive about her affairs. Unless she got into a jam and needed help, I really didn't know much about the men she dated."

"Did your help include previous pregnancies?"

"No, not that." She didn't want to get into details—some were rather sordid—so she tried to change the slant of the conversation before he went any further.

"So you think the Arabic name on the boat doesn't mean anything significant?" she asked.

"It might or might not. We're handicapped by not really knowing anything about this man."

The roughness in his voice alerted her. "You're angry with him, aren't you?"

"Who wouldn't be? I know you are."

"Yes," she agreed, "but Erin was my cousin and my friend. I realize it takes two to get pregnant, but I can't help but believe if it hadn't been for him, she'd still be alive. Maybe he couldn't have saved her, but at the very least he could have stood by her through it all. That's not your reason for being angry."

He leaned forward, looking at her. "I didn't know Erin but I know you. He's blighted your life. Now he's interfering in mine. I can't explain the blood match between Danny and me—I can only try to prove to you that I couldn't have been Erin's lover. Is that possible where you're concerned? Or will there always remain the shadow of doubt? You know as well as I do that he's come between us, and there he'll stay until we find him. I hate the bastard!''

The ferocity in his voice took her aback.

"Then there's Danny," he continued. "What's going to happen to him?''

"I'll take good care of him," she said defensively. "I love Danny!''

"Boys need fathers, too.''

Yes, she thought, *and you'd make a good one for him. If only you'd been the man in the picture and hadn't known about Erin's pregnancy I think I could forgive you, because I can see you're beginning to love Danny.* She started to chew on her thumbnail as what he'd called the shadow of doubt loomed darkly.

Should she believe him? Had he and Jade conspired to lie to her? The Reno lab would be sending the DNA report to her San Diego address as soon as they received it. What if that, as well as the blood, was a match?

"Karen," he said. "Look at me.''

She didn't want to; she couldn't bring herself to.

He rose and pulled her to her feet. Hands on her shoulders, he repeated his command. "Look at me!''

Bracing herself so she wouldn't make the mistake of falling into his dark gaze again, she took a deep breath and did as he asked. The pain she saw in his eyes twisted her heart.

"I swear I've never lied to you." His voice throbbed with emotion. "I am not Danny's father.''

She wanted to believe him; she needed to believe him. She longed to put her arms around him and offer him comfort, more than comfort. But he was right—the man in the photo, whoever he was, stood between them.

"We'll keep searching," she said finally. It was all she could offer him.

When Zed, bitter and frustrated, reached his hotel room, the red light on his phone was blinking. The message the desk gave him turned out to be from George Stone, a request to meet him at the marina at seven in the morning. Which probably meant, Zed realized, that good old George had decided to trust him with the *Painted Lady* for the duration of his stay.

He wished he could sail her out of the bay into the ocean and keep going until the sea and the sun and the wind blew away what his grandma had referred to as the bogies.

"Everybody has them," she'd told Zed when he was young. "Your grandpa and I do, just like you. Sometimes they seemed about to devour us but here we still are, so you can be sure you're safe."

He sat on the bed, untying his running shoes and kicking them off. His socks went, then the rest of his clothes. He lay on the bed naked, feeling slightly better with San Diego's moist sea air cool on his skin. His grandparents had always seemed so together that he wondered what bogies had haunted them.

He recalled how upset his grandmother used to get when he or Jade failed to come directly home from school, forgetting to call to say they'd stopped at a friend's house or some such on the way. That seemed pretty normal, though, considering she was old to be raising kids and had already lost her only child, Jade's and his mother.

His grandparents had many pictures of Ellen Marie Adams as a baby, a toddler, growing into a teen. Jade looked quite a bit like her, even to the green eyes. There hadn't been any pictures of his mother's wedding, though, and not a single photo of his father. His early questions had been silenced by his grandmother saying, "He's dead and we don't talk about him. It was your mother's wish, as it was her wish that you and Jade take her maiden name when we adopted you. Our name."

He knew his dark hair and eyes came from his father, because Grandpa had let that slip once. He'd always wanted to know more about the man who'd fathered him, and when he was in his twenties he'd confronted his grandfather. "Is my father really dead?" he'd asked.

Grandpa had looked him in the eye. "Have I ever lied to you?"

Zed had to admit Bill Adams was as honest as they came. His grandfather might hold back information, but he wouldn't deliberately lie.

"What my mother asked you and Grandma to do," he'd persisted, "was to obliterate my father. Even his name. Why?"

"Ellen Marie had her reasons. We did as she asked. That's all I can tell you."

"But they *were* married?"

"They were married. Now I think we've discussed the matter enough." At that point Grandpa had risen from the kitchen stool and left the house, effectively ending the conversation. Zed had never brought it up again.

After his grandparents passed away, he'd searched for a marriage certificate or other papers, hoping to at least learn what his father's name had been. He found nothing relevant.

His birth certificate and Jade's were no help, since they listed his grandparents rather than his mother and father as the parents, something he'd always wondered about. That, too, had been explained as his mother's request, just as she had insisted her parents legally adopt her children.

He'd been curious and had never had his curiosity satisfied, but he'd been forced by his grandparents' persistent silence to let things ride. Not until this moment, though, had it occurred to him to wonder if his father had ever had a child in or out of wedlock before he met Ellen Marie Adams. A son who'd be a man now. A son who looked a lot like the one he'd fathered with Ellen Adams. Like Zed.

He shook his head. Enough speculation. He needed solid facts if he was ever going to find Danny's father.

Chapter Five

Morning mist obscured the bay and the marina when Zed met George Stone at seven in the morning.

"Texans are prone to trades," George told him, getting right to the point. "Here's what I'm proposing. I can't take *Painted Lady* out by myself these days. She's always been a handful for one man, and my wife isn't able to crew for me like she used to. Damn arthritis slows a man down. I can't move quick anymore. So, you take me out for a sail a couple times a week and you can use the boat for your stay here."

"That's a hell of an offer," Zed said. "You do realize you're rewarding me for using the *Painted Lady*."

George shrugged. "You get what you want, I get what I want. Deal?"

"Deal." Zed shook George's hand.

"One more thing," George said. "After we met yesterday, I watched you for a while and for the life of me I couldn't figure out what you were up to. Looked like casual conversations here and there, but I saw they weren't. Asking questions, that's what you were doing. None of my business, but I'm a nosy old goat. Checked you out later, too. You're what you said you were and well thought of up there in the boondocks, to boot. To me it didn't add up—a Nevada rancher roaming the marina asking questions. Just what the hell are you doing here in San Diego?''

No reason not to tell George. ''I'm hunting for a man who looks like me,'' Zed said. ''Chances are he owns a thirty-two-foot clipper named *Maddamti,* because I have a photo of him on board that particular boat. The *Star of India*'s in the background, so San Diego is where this picture was taken a year ago last summer.'' Zed pulled out his copy of the photo and showed it to George. ''I need to get in touch with him and this is all I have to go on.''

After a careful examination, George shook his head. ''Nothing familiar here. Sorry. But I'll keep it in mind. Got a lot of old sailor buddies. I'll ask around.''

''Thanks.'' Zed handed him the photo, saying, ''Keep this to show your friends. I have another.'' He added, ''When do we go for our first sail?''

George glanced around at the persistent mist still obscuring the bay. ''Not today, obviously. Supposed to rain tomorrow, but we can try for Sunday. You call me.'' He handed his card to Zed along with the boat keys and a cellular phone. ''This belongs on the boat. Use it while you're there. We'd have coffee somewhere but Doc has made me swear off caffeine and I can't stand that other muck. Talk to you on Sunday."

Elated at temporarily acquiring a shipshape boat like George's, Zed returned to the motel to move his things to the *Painted Lady*. Remembering he ought to let Karen know, he punched in her number.

"Hello?" Her voice sounded harried.

Zed started to tell her about his change of address, but she interrupted him.

"I can't talk right now 'cause I need to use the phone. Danny's regular sitter called in sick and I'm desperately trying to find another sitter for him. I hate to miss any more time, especially today, because I'm supposed to chair the monthly meeting."

"You found one," Zed said.

"What?"

"A sitter. Me."

"You? But you can't—"

"Why not?" he demanded. "Tiger knows me and I know him. We'll get along just fine without you for a few hours. I'll be over in fifteen minutes or so, depending on traffic." He hung up without waiting for her to agree or disagree.

He checked out of the motel, piled his belongings into the car and took off for La Mesa.

When he reached her apartment, a harried Karen thrust the boy at him, at the same time showering him with multiple instructions—changing diapers, when to feed Danny, when he napped, where the emergency numbers were. At that point he stopped her.

"Relax. I'll cope. Trust me."

She chewed on her thumbnail. "I'd like to, but taking

care of a baby isn't as easy as you think. Maybe I shouldn't go to work.''

"Go, already," he said. "Tiger isn't crying—he's glad to see me. He'll let me know when he needs to eat or sleep or be changed. What's the problem?"

"You don't have the slightest idea what you're doing," she told him. "But you're right—Danny will survive." She smiled slightly. "I'm not so sure about you."

After issuing more instructions, she finally left, returning almost immediately to give him Danny's car seat in case he needed to use it.

After that, still toting Danny, he waved her off. "Women," he told the boy, who was eyeing him uncertainly. "You're still too young to realize what worrywarts they can be."

Danny's lower lip began to quiver and Zed cast a hasty look around for the blue horse with the bedraggled ears. Where the hell was it? By the time he located the blasted horse in the crib in the bedroom the boy shared with Karen, Danny was whimpering.

Spotting a rocker in the living room, he dropped into it, shifted the boy in his arms, handed him the horse and began rocking. Danny hugged the horse but continued to whimper. "I'd sing to you, Tiger," he muttered, "but I can't carry a tune for—" He stopped abruptly, realizing he was on the verge of corrupting the baby's innocent ears with a four-letter word.

"How about if I whistle?" he asked. "Think you'd like that?" He pursed his lips and started off with the first tune that popped into his head, a country-western song he couldn't remember the name of, something to do with a guy who was crying in his beer. He was well launched into the tune when the boy stopped fussing and twisted around to watch him. A moment later he began poking a finger between Zed's pursed lips, interfering with the whistle.

Reminded of games he'd watched his grandparents play with Jade—maybe they had with him, too, but he didn't recall it—he leaned over, grabbed a pillow off the couch and started playing peek a boo. This simple maneuver amused Danny far longer than it did Zed. Finally unable to peek another boo, he hefted the boy around the waist and stood him on his feet.

"Da!" Danny exclaimed, bending his knees and then straightening them. "Da, da."

"Like that, do you? Told you you'd be walking in no time." Rising from the rocker, he sat on the floor, still holding the boy erect. Danny bounced happily up and down until Zed's arms got tired.

He pulled an afghan off the couch, spread it on the carpeted floor, sat Danny on the afghan and rolled a large red ball he'd found in the playpen toward him. Danny squealed with glee when the ball bumped against his leg. He didn't have a clue how to roll it back, so Zed retrieved the ball and rolled it at Danny again. When that palled— at least, as far as he was concerned—he tried out other toys that clicked or rang or clacked, temporarily as fascinated by their ingenuity as the boy was.

When nature called, he decided for safety's sake to sit the boy in the playpen while he went to the bathroom. He hadn't taken more than two steps away before Danny let out a horrendous howl.

"Okay, Tiger," Zed said, scooping him up. "I suppose

you might as well come with me and see how it's done for future reference.''

Careful maneuvering enabled him to relieve himself without dropping Danny into the toilet. On the way back he discovered that whether or not the kid's diaper had been wet before the trip to the bathroom, it certainly was sopping now.

He remembered Karen explaining that she kept the changing table in the bedroom because the bathroom was too small. ''Here goes nothing,'' he said as he laid the boy on his back on the table. Seeing the stack of clean disposable diapers at hand, he added, ''Easy as falling off a fence, right?''

Which it might have been if Danny had lain there quietly instead of squirming all over the table so that he had to be pinned firmly with one hand to keep him in place while, with the other hand, the outer pants had to be tugged off before the wet diaper could be unfastened and dropped into a nearby pail. Then came the tricky part. How the hell was anyone expected to get a clean diaper on a wriggling eel whose aim was plain—to see how quickly he could manage to fall off the table?

Zed sighed in relief when he managed to get the diaper fastened, no matter that it looked a tad crooked. Since the outer pants, miniature jeans, seemed damp, he picked Danny up while he looked for a clean pair.

''You know,'' he confided, ''there's a lot to be said for running around naked. Wouldn't work too good inside, not till you're housebroken, but outside it'd be a breeze.''

At that point he recalled his afternoon appointment with the P.I., and flipped Danny up onto his shoulder while he called Joe Santoro's office. Danny slid down, trying his best to punch the phone buttons right along with him, but Zed got the call through without too much trouble.

He explained that he was baby-sitting. "I could bring the boy with me," he said, "but I think he takes a nap about that time."

"I know where Karen lives," Joe said. "How about if I come out after lunch? I got another call to make in La Mesa, anyway."

That seemed the best arrangement to Zed. Joe's mention of lunch reminded him that the coffee and doughnut he'd had for breakfast was long gone, so, even though it was only eleven, he opted to eat. Karen had said there was leftover pizza in the refrigerator that he could heat in the microwave, which sounded good to him. The poor kid was probably getting hungry, too, since he seemed kind of restless.

Luckily he'd had recent experience with the baby food jars in Nevada and had watched Karen feed the boy. He figured it'd be a cinch to combine feeding Danny with eating his own lunch. That was mistake number one. He didn't realize how messy the process could be, nor did he recall how the kid had kept trying to grab the spoon. Handing Danny a spoon of his own to hold didn't improve matters, because he was determined to stick the spoon into the pizza slices Zed was trying to eat. Too late he recalled Karen telling him the high chair was stored in the pantry.

Still, they finished their lunches without a real disaster. That came later. Either Karen hadn't had time to mention that certain bodily processes were activated in Danny after eating or else he hadn't listened closely. Mistake number two turned out to be leaving the diaper cockeyed rather than making sure it was on correctly. Combined with not getting around to putting outer pants over the askew diaper, this led to some mighty odoriferous leakage. On him, the kitchen chair, the floor and all over Danny.

He stripped Danny and, seeing nothing else available in sight, grabbed paper towels and more or less mummified him. He wiped the worst of the stuff off his pants so he wouldn't drip on his way and made tracks for the bathroom. Confronted by a too-small sink and a shower within a tub, he groaned. After deciding against the tub—it would take too long to fill—he stripped himself, turned on the shower, making sure it wasn't too hot, and stepped under it with Danny in his arms, hoping the kid wouldn't set up a howl.

The paper towels grew sodden and peeled off under the water's onslaught, stopping up the drain so that Zed had to keep pushing disintegrating paper aside with his foot while he kept a grip on the slippery boy and tried to wash him clean at the same time. Because he'd forgotten to close the shower's sliding doors, the entire bathroom was awash by the time he finished. The only redeeming factor besides cleanliness was that he hadn't scared Danny.

Once he'd gotten them dry, he retrieved a new diaper, shirt and outer pants and dressed the kid. He then hauled the high chair into the hall and put the boy in it with one of his cookies, leaving the bathroom door open so he could keep an eye on Danny. Examining his clothes, Zed saw his jeans and boxers would have to be soaked in lieu of washing. His T-shirt, while not smelly, was dotted with various colors of baby food. Everything he'd worn needed a wash.

After laying towels on the floor to sop up the water and picking soggy paper towels out of the drain, Zed ran water into the tub, added some dish detergent from the kitchen and dropped his clothes in to soak. After a moment's thought, he added Danny's soiled shirt and socks. Not knowing what to do with the dirty diaper, he tied it into a plastic bag.

"I have clean clothes in the car," he told Danny, giving a rueful glance at his nakedness. "You got any idea how I'm going to get out there to collect them without shocking the neighbors?"

Danny had no suggestions to offer. The only possibility, Zed decided, was to tie a towel around his waist. This being Southern California, maybe no one would raise an eyebrow. Before he ventured out, he brought Danny, high chair and all, into the kitchen and cleaned up the mess there. Then he discovered that the only remaining towel large enough to cover him decently was bright pink with purple flowers. By now he really didn't care. Afraid to leave Danny alone while he went out to the car, he hoisted him from the high chair and carried him along.

He reached his car, unfortunately parked on the street rather than within the apartment complex, grabbed jeans and a shirt and was closing the door when a nondescript black car pulled up behind it. A stocky man got out and stared at him.

"You must be Adams," he said.

"What makes you think so?" Zed asked gruffly.

"I recognize the kid." He smiled at Danny, who turned his face into Zed's shoulder. "I'm Joe Santoro. Looks like you got your hands full—we can shake hands later."

Joe followed him back to Karen's apartment. Zed left him in the living room while he retreated to the bedroom with Danny, remembering to pick up the blue horse on the way. He deposited boy and horse in the crib, pulling a blanket up around them both. "I'll stay in here with you while I get dressed, Tiger," he said, "but after that you and Old Blue are on your own. Enough is enough."

Danny, the horse's ear in his mouth, watched him drowsily. To Zed's relief the boy's eyes drooped shut and didn't pop open when he eased out the door.

"Planning to take up baby-sitting as a sideline?" Joe asked when he reached the living room.

"Comedy must be *your* sideline," Zed muttered.

"Let's see if I got this right," Joe said. "I pegged you for the kid's father, but you've convinced Karen you can prove you're not."

"It's the truth."

"Okay, let's say you're *not* Danny's father. I got to tell you that, in my eyes, you're acting a hell of a lot like you are."

Zed tamped down his irritation. No point in antagonizing Joe. On the other hand he refused to be defensive about sitting with Danny. "I came to San Diego to find the man you mistook me for," he said. "What I'd like from you is a rundown of your investigation for Karen, so that I don't duplicate your efforts."

"She signed a release, so here goes." Joe launched into a detailed report of what Karen had already told Zed in capsule form.

"The woman who identified me from the photo," Zed said when Joe had finished. "Why was she so sure the man was me?"

"Apparently you took her and a couple of her girl-friends out for a sail maybe two or three years ago. I guess you impressed her, 'cause she sure as hell remembered every detail, including your name and the fact you lived in Nevada. Plus your buns.''

Zed didn't have the slightest recollection of the incident, but he often invited new acquaintances sailing, people he might never see again.

"How about the redhead—Erin?" Zed asked. "Did this woman know her?"

Joe shook his head. "Never set eyes on her. Claimed she never saw you with the redhead, either."

About to ask the woman's name and where he could contact her, Zed hesitated. What was the point? If she believed the man in the photo was him, she'd be of no help whatsoever. "Thanks, Joe," he said. "I appreciate you coming out here."

"Better a bawling kid at home than in my office."

"Tiger's a good kid. He doesn't fuss without reason," Zed said before he thought.

Joe rolled his eyes. "Sure you ain't his father? Believe me, you sound like it."

Goaded, Zed spoke between his teeth. "I never met Erin Henderson. Or donated sperm. I'm no one's father."

"If you say so, man. Me, I'm just a bystander. Karen's a nice lady, though." He eyed Zed. "Too nice to get hurt."

Fighting not to let his anger loose—what did Joe think he was, some sleazy son of a bitch who went around impregnating women and then deserting them?—Zed said tautly, "Goodbye and thanks again, Joe."

Zed had originally thought he might mention the possibility his father had sired another son before marrying Ellen Adams, but he'd decided not to. The P.I.'s investigation had labeled him as the father, and Joe's mind-set remained fixed on that. Even if he had brought up the possibility, Joe most likely would have pointed out the futility of trying to find a half brother who might not exist when he didn't even know his father's name.

After the P.I. had gone, Zed put some finishing touches on the kitchen. In the bathroom he rinsed the clothes in the bathtub, wrung them out and dropped Danny's into the hamper. His he stuffed into a plastic bag. After wiping up a few stray damp spots, he deposited the wet towels in the hamper, too, stood back and gazed with satisfaction at his cleanup job. He'd successfully remedied his mistakes. Unless some nosy neighbor had spotted him outside clad in the floral towel, Karen would never suspect anything had gone amiss.

The doorbell rang. Zed hurried to answer it, not wanting Danny to rouse. He peered through the spy-eye before opening the door and blinked at the sight of a uniformed cop on the other side. What was this?

Even though she chaired it, the afternoon meeting passed in a blur for Karen. The kids had been dismissed shortly after noon because of the meeting, so actually she'd be leaving earlier than usual but, for the moment, she was stuck here.

All she could think about was getting away and hurrying home to see if Danny was all right. When she'd called before the meeting began, Zed hadn't answered even after ten rings. Where had he been? He and Danny, that is, because surely he wouldn't leave a baby alone. She hadn't had a chance to get to the phone again and the suspense was taking its toll.

She trusted Zed, she told herself over and over. He was

perfectly capable of taking care of a seven-month-old boy. Many fathers did as well or better at child care than the mothers. But Zed wasn't Danny's father, or at least most of the time she believed he wasn't, and he hadn't had any experience taking care of babies.

She'd learned, she reminded herself, and Danny was a newborn then. He was seven months older now, and Zed was an intelligent man. If there'd been an emergency, he would have called. If he'd decided to go for a drive, he had the car seat for Danny.

Finally she was able to bring the meeting to a close. She flew to her car and broke a few speed limits on the way to her apartment. She sighed with relief when she spotted Zed's rental car parked in the same place. He hadn't gone anywhere—she'd find him and Danny where she'd left them. Everything was fine and dandy.

Then, pulling in to her assigned slot in the complex, she noticed a patrol car in the guest parking area and her heart began to pound. Imagining all sorts of calamities, she leapt out of her car and raced to her apartment. She burst inside and stopped short.

Zed sat in the kitchen with Danny in his lap. The boy had a cookie in his left hand and his blue horse clutched in his right.

In the chair opposite Zed a young and pretty uniformed policewoman was just setting down her cup of coffee, her gaze on Karen. She rose and said, "You must be Ms. Henderson. I'm Officer Kelly, La Mesa Police Department. I've been waiting for you to get here."

Her wits still scattered, Karen mumbled a greeting and crossed to Zed, reaching for Danny.

He smiled at her but resisted when she tried to pick him up, hanging on to Zed. "Da!" he said. "Da!"

"As I explained to Mr. Adams," the officer said, "I'm sorry to have bothered you but we received a complaint from a resident of this complex telling us she'd noticed a naked man outside with your baby, and this man had let another man into your apartment. Since she'd never seen either of the men before, she was afraid they were up to no good—especially the naked one."

Was Officer Kelly suppressing a smile? It looked very much like it to Karen. She could understand that the police had to respond to a call, but why did this one, whose uniform accentuated her blond attractiveness, have to hang around and drink coffee with Zed? And what was this about nakedness?

"When she rang the doorbell it woke up Tiger," Zed interjected, "and he began to howl. We had a few interesting minutes before I managed to convince Lucy I was a perfectly innocent baby-sitter."

Lucy? How long had the officer been here?

"Yes, you're very convincing," Karen snapped before she could stop herself. Recovering, she managed to say, "There really is nothing to worry about, Officer."

Officer Kelly nodded. "Since there's no problem here, I'll be leaving. You two have a good day." She waved at Danny. Or was it Zed? "Bye-bye, cutie."

Danny offered her a tentative smile, then—belatedly—held out his arms to Karen. She plucked him off Zed's lap, cuddling him next to her.

"Goodbye, Lucy," Zed said. "May all your calls be as harmless as this one."

The officer gave Zed a big smile, nodded to Karen and let herself out.

Karen stood with her back against the refrigerator, frowning at Zed. "What was that all about?" she demanded.

"You have at least one nosy neighbor with a vivid imagination. A man wearing a towel wrapped around his significant parts is definitely not naked."

For the first time Karen noticed that he wore a red T-shirt, and she was certain he'd had on a white one when he'd arrived, a shirt with a casino logo—a rose in the barrel of a gun, as she recalled. And these were faded jeans, not the darker ones he'd worn earlier.

Avoiding Danny's persistent attempts to feed her his cookie, she shook her head. "Maybe you'd better start at the beginning."

"The other man was Joe Santoro," he said. "He came by instead of me going to his office. Tiger was never in the slightest danger."

"I can understand Joe coming here," she said, "but what were you doing outside wearing nothing but a towel and, apparently, carrying Danny?"

"I couldn't leave him alone in the apartment, so I had no choice. Look, why don't you get comfortable and I'll explain what happened."

Discovering that he'd dropped his blue horse onto the floor when Karen picked him up, Danny twisted in her arms, trying to get free and reach for his favorite toy. Zed retrieved the horse and Danny lunged toward him. Sighing, Karen handed him back to Zed. Kicking off her shoes, she collected a soft drink from the refrigerator and dropped into a chair.

"Okay," she said, "I'm as comfortable as I'm able to be until I hear a blow-by-blow account of your day with Danny."

Tense and inclined to be annoyed at first, Karen felt her sense of humor rapidly take hold as what Zed called his mistakes piled one onto the other. By the time he got to the paper towels clogging up the drain, she was chuckling. When he told her about the pink towel with purple flowers, she laughed until tears came to her eyes.

"Mrs. Hammond," Karen said when she could speak. "She watches us all, so she had to be the one who called the cops. But who can blame her? What a sight you must have been. How I wish I could have seen Joe confronting you down in the street. God only knows what he thought."

"He wanted to know if I intended to make a career out of baby-sitting," Zed told her. "Some comedian. Tiger never batted an eye through it all, though. Not even in the shower."

"His first, incidentally."

"So what are we going to do for dinner? If you don't have any other plans, we could eat on the *Painted Lady*. How does that strike you?"

She raised her eyebrows. "I think you've left something out, because I haven't the slightest idea what you're talking about."

"Didn't I tell you? My new address is a sailboat moored in the marina. A Texas gentleman lent it to me."

"Great! But maybe not tonight, okay? If Danny's nap was interrupted he's going to zonk out early." Zed looked so disappointed that she added, "Why don't we plan to picnic on the boat tomorrow instead?"

"Good enough. I'll go out and bring something back for dinner."

She ought to discourage him; he was on the way to becoming a fixture in her life, and that would never do. "You needn't bother," she began, trying to find a tactful way to put it, which was doubly difficult because she really didn't want him to go.

"You mean you'd rather have homemade?" he asked before she found the right words to suggest he leave. "I noticed some spaghetti in the cupboard when I took out the baby food. My one and only cooking talent besides French toast is spaghetti sauce. If you've got the makings for it, go put your feet up and I'll make dinner."

Karen gave in. Leaving him pulling out pans in the kitchen, she carried Danny with her into the bedroom to change into more casual clothes. Somehow the old jeans and white T-shirt she'd meant to wear turned into rust-colored knit pants with a long overshirt of the same color, an outfit she knew flattered her coloring. She took extra pains with her hair.

Danny, watching her from his crib, began to babble. "Ma!" he said, among other syllables. "Ma, ma."

"It's about time you got around to that," she told him as she lifted him up. "I'm getting tired of this 'Da' business."

The meal went well. Danny drooped early and eased into sleep without fussing. Which left her alone with Zed in the living room. "TV?" she said a bit too brightly.

He shook his head. "I need to talk to you. I couldn't mention this to Joe Santoro because he's convinced he didn't make a mistake, that I have to be the man in the picture. But let me run this past you and see what you think.''

Karen sat in amazement as he told her how his grandparents had refused to give him any information about his father. When he got to the possibility of a half brother, she had to admit it would explain the resemblance, and maybe the blood match.

''But how can you ever find out?'' she asked when he was finished.

Zed sighed. ''That's the problem. All I can think of at this point is to hang around the marina.''

He looked so discouraged that she got up from her chair and moved to the couch, where he was sitting. At that moment she had no doubts about him, none at all. Putting her hand on his shoulder, she said, ''If he exists, you'll find him. If he doesn't, I'm convinced you'll still discover who the man in the photo is.''

He turned to her, his dark gaze holding her captive. ''Joe warned me not to hurt you,'' he said. ''I wish I could promise I won't.'' And then he kissed her.

Chapter Six

Relaxing once she discovered Danny was safe and sound, Karen had found herself enjoying Zed's presence. Never had her apartment seemed so welcoming. Basking in the friendly easiness of sharing simple tasks, she'd felt it was almost as though the three of them were a family.

Her imagination had pursued that thought. If they really *were* a family, Zed wouldn't be getting into his car and driving to the marina tonight—they'd be sharing a bed. That realization had sent a tingle along her spine as she'd imagined cuddling into his embrace. The image had stayed with her as she listened to his concern over whether or not they'd ever find Danny's father, and it had accompanied her from the chair to the couch when she'd joined him there in order to offer encouragement.

When he looked at her, she knew what would happen, but she did nothing to avoid his kiss. Instead of backing off, she melted into his arms, mingling the real with the fantasy. *This is where I belong,* she thought. *I belong with Zed, held close to him, his lips on mine.*

Did he feel the same way? Did he have this same sensation of oneness? She cut her wondering short, reminding herself their feelings couldn't be compared, because they were different—she was a woman and he was a man.

Was he ever a man! Never had anyone aroused her in the manner he did. His lips, warm and compelling, urged her to abandon herself to the magic sizzling between them. His touch, skimming her breasts with a teasing caress, started her spiraling up and up, wanting more, needing more, caught in an erotic thermal of desire.

Enveloped in his clean, masculine scent, savoring his taste, her fingers entwined in his soft, dark curls, she longed to become a part of him. There might be reasons that she shouldn't make love with him but, bemused as she was by his caresses, reasons didn't matter.

"Zed, oh, Zed," she murmured against his lips, all her longing translated into his name.

"Karen," he whispered. "My beautiful Karen." His lips trailed along her throat, making her quiver from the tingling deep inside.

He'd called her his. She hadn't even considered that she might one day feel she belonged to any man, but she did right now. She *was* his. Completely his. And, for the moment, he was hers.

His hand slipped under her shirt to mold her breast through her bra. A tiny moan escaped her as his thumb slid over her nipple.

Pulling slightly away from her, he said, "If you want me to stop, it has to be now. You have to tell me now."

His voice, roughened by passion, increased the fire within her.

She didn't want him to stop. Ever. And yet his words made her realize she was letting her emotions overpower her sense. Her body ruled, not her mind. Making love with Zed was not a good idea. Not while this uncertainty about him plagued her.

Sighing, she eased free. "We stop," she said.

Letting her go completely, he nodded, then got to his feet. "Much as I want to stay, I'm off to my temporary home on the boat. Now."

At the door she made a quick agreement to meet him at the marina around ten. "With a full picnic basket," she added.

"Rain or shine?" he asked.

"Rain won't stop us. My mother taught me young that I won't melt, and I'm teaching the same thing to Danny."

He leaned to her and her breath caught as she waited for his kiss. Instead, he touched the palm of his hand to her cheek. And then he was gone.

She took a deep breath and leaned against the closed door. So much for staying uninvolved. Not only had she and Zed advanced well along the lovemaking path but, if she didn't know better, she'd say that earlier today she'd actually been jealous of Officer Lucy Kelly.

After transferring his belongings to the boat, Zed decided that, even though it was barely ten, he'd call it a day. He was tired—taking care of a baby was a hell of a lot tougher than he'd imagined. He called his sister to let her know about his new quarters, but she wasn't home, so he left a message on her answering machine. Yawning, he crawled into the bunk and zonked out.

Feeling as alone as he'd ever been in his life, he walked through mist that hid his surroundings, making it impossible to orient himself. Although he had no idea where he was, he knew he must go on. Somewhere in the grayness was what he searched for. When he found it, whatever it was, he'd never be alone again.

How was he to find anything in this alien mist? His chances must be close to zero. Never mind the odds, the alternative was to remain incomplete, so he had no choice but to blunder on, even if it took forever.

Suddenly the terrain changed, only the mist remaining. Instead of solid ground under his feet, he felt the heaving deck of a boat weathering a blow. He was not at the tiller. Was anyone steering, or was he adrift, at the mercy of the wind? He thought he heard the deep bellow of a foghorn but, as he strained his ears to locate the direction, the sound grew fainter, changing to a chant of meaningless syllables.

He became convinced he was aboard the Maddamti *and that he must reach the tiller before disaster struck. The thick mist and the unsteady footing on the constantly tilting deck hampered his search, confusing him until he lost his sense of fore and aft. The clang of warning buoys tensed him. Out of the mist a voice spoke, neuter, neither male nor female.*

"You're on the wrong boat," the voice said.

Of course he was—the Maddamti *wasn't his—but in this fog how was he to find the right boat? Or land. Or anything?*

Lost, he was lost....

Zed woke with a start, for a moment not sure where he was. The gentle rocking beneath him, the slap of water against the hull and the patter of rain on wood above his head told him he was on a boat and that it was raining. Logic insisted he was in San Diego, so the boat had to be the *Painted Lady,* but shards of the dream cluttered his mind, disturbing him.

Don't sweat it, he advised himself. The dream came from the boat rocking while he slept and the fact that he was here on a search. Or on a wild-goose chase, depending on how he looked at it. Yet the dream had a haunting familiarity, reminding him of others he'd had in the past. With an effort he threw off the dream's cobwebs.

The gray light creeping through the portholes assured him it was morning, His watch said seven. He stretched and locked his hands behind his head, savoring the familiar feel of a boat moving beneath him, a sensation he truly enjoyed. If he ever did make love to Karen, he thought, here was the appropriate place.

Except making love to her anywhere was not a good idea. When he found the man in the photo, everything would be different. *If* he found the man...

Rather than lying around bogging down his mind with negative possibilities, Zed slid from the bunk and pulled on his clothes. Coffee time.

As he'd expected, the marina was deserted. Nothing like rain to dampen a sailor's enthusiasm. Accustomed to dropping in to a casino on the rare occasions when he ate breakfast out—casinos always offered fantastic meals at giveaway prices—he had to adjust his thinking to California prices when he found a café.

As a recent graduate to nonsmoking, he appreciated the

clean air, though. The casinos still catered to smokers, and it was doubly hard to find he still yearned to light one up at the same time that he was resenting having to breathe secondhand smoke.

After he ate, to kill time until Karen arrived, he found a Laundromat and washed and dried his dirty clothes from the previous day. While he was there, one of the little kids running loose waiting for their mothers slipped and fell in front of him.

Seeing that the boy was undecided whether to cry or not, Zed realized he couldn't be hurt. He picked him up and set him on his feet, noting the logo on his T-shirt. "What happened, Batman," he said, "is that you forgot your cape. You know that cape keeps you from taking a fall?"

The kid stared at him, digesting this, all thought of crying forgotten, then ran to find his mother. Zed smiled. In a few months Danny would be running around, too.

The woman putting clothes in the dryer next to his said, "I can tell you're a father. Single guys don't pay any attention to kids."

Rather than set her straight, he nodded politely, pulled his clothes from the dryer, slung them over his arm and exited. A father? He shook his head. No, not him. That was the guy he had to find.

Karen arrived a few minutes before ten, both she and Danny encased in plastic rainproofing. She ducked into the cabin, set down the picnic basket on the table and handed Danny to him. "You can peel him out of that slicker while I get rid of mine," she said.

He sat on one of the benches by the table, enjoying her ease with him—she hadn't bothered to say please. As if he really was the kid's father and she was the mother, as if they belonged together.

Once Danny was free of his rainproofing, he twisted around and poked his finger into Zed's mouth. "Da?" he said.

"He wants you to do something," Karen translated, "but I haven't the slightest idea what."

After a moment's thought Zed recalled how he'd whistled to the boy the day before. He launched into "Barnacle Bill the Sailor." Danny grinned, rocking back and forth on his lap.

"Oh, great," Karen said. "Now he'll probably expect me to do it, and I can't whistle for shucks." She glanced around. "Rather close quarters, but nice. Very nice."

"She's a beautiful boat," Zed said, abandoning the whistling, at the same time handing Danny a toy he'd bought in a novelty store on the way back to the boat— a rubber duck that quacked when squeezed.

Noting what he'd done, Karen said, "You catch on fast."

"The kid's a good teacher. I've learned a lot about distraction techniques. Now, about the boat. I'm taking her owner sailing tomorrow if the weather clears. There's plenty of room for you and Danny—why don't you come along? George won't mind."

"Maybe. Let me think about it." She pointed to the made-up bunk. "Is that where you sleep?"

He nodded and said, "Where I slept and dreamed. A really strange one." He regretted the confession as soon as the words were out. Dreams were meant to be kept private, not aired abroad to bore everyone except maybe shrinks.

"I dreamed, too." Almost immediately Karen flushed, looking as though she wished she could take the admission back.

Her reaction gave her away. Hoping he'd been the man involved, he smiled, wishing his dream had been an erotic one with Karen in it instead of a near nightmare.

They talked and played with Danny until he decided he was hungry. Once fed and changed, the boy grew drowsy. Karen laid him on the bunk and Zed made a barricade of pillows to keep him from rolling off.

"It's cosy in here," Karen said, "with the rain drumming on the roof. No, not the roof—what's above us is called the deck, isn't it? And this rocking motion is so soothing I feel like crawling in beside Danny and taking a nap. Not that you're putting me to sleep," she added hastily.

He grinned across the table at her. "Must be the sandman's come aboard, because I was just thinking about a nap myself." He didn't add that nap might not be exactly the right word, though he was certainly interested in lying down. With Karen in his arms.

"Would you like another cookie?" she asked, pushing the plate toward him.

"Thanks." He took one, saying, "Poor Tiger, forced to eat those bland things when you make chocolate chip cookies to die for. I notice you put oatmeal in them like my grandmother used to do. It's the only way."

"Healthier," she told him. "Or so I try to convince myself when I eat too many. Erin was allergic to chocolate, so I intend to keep it away from Danny as long as possible in case he inherited her sensitivity." She sighed.

"I miss her, and I feel sad that she didn't live to watch her son grow and thrive."

"From what you've told me, Erin seemed to be one of those people who live for the moment, letting the future take care of itself. Do you think she'd have made a good mother?"

"People do change," she said defensively.

"Not a lot, once they're adults. If your cousin had lived, I'll bet she'd have parked Danny with you half the time."

"Probably," Karen admitted. "Unless she contacted his father and he took over."

"He's out there somewhere," Zed said. "Erin, though, had the advantage of knowing his name. We don't."

Why was he going on about Erin and the search for Danny's father? What he wanted, what he needed was Karen. In his arms. In his bed. Which they'd have to share with Danny at the moment. Inconvenient, if not impossible. And that was just as well.

Partly to distract himself and partly because he was truly interested, he asked her about teaching, working backward to her earlier life.

"You're lucky to have a sister not too far removed in age," she said after she'd talked for a while about her family. "You and Jade can share things. My half brother, Steve—Dad's son by his first wife, who died—is twelve years older than I am. We're friends, but the age gap was too great for us to become close. Without asking if I needed any, Steve sent money to help me out when I came back from the Caribbean with Danny. He's never uttered one word of criticism about me taking Danny, either."

"Sounds like one of the good guys."

She nodded. "Actually, he's the only male I know who didn't take Erin up on her offer when she came on to him. I don't know that she ever spoke to him again. She hated rejection. Of course, she *was* only fifteen at the time."

"She must have started young."

"From the cradle, my dad used to say. But I think he and my mom both knew Erin was really looking for love and thought she could find it in sex. You can't, you know."

Was she referring to them? Her blue eyes, gazing at him, seemed guileless. "There's nothing wrong with sex," he said, "providing the two people involved have enough sense to recognize the dangers."

"And they don't mistake sex for love," she added.

"That, too," he conceded, wondering if she was offering a subtle warning about them, a warning whose meaning wasn't quite clear. No sex without love? Or was it don't expect love with sex?

He didn't need the warning. He'd loved his grandparents, he loved his sister but, looking back at the girls and women he'd been attracted to, he couldn't say he'd been in love with any of them. He hadn't expected any of them to love him, either, though some had claimed they did. As for no sex without love—he shook his head, not caring to touch that with a ten-foot pole.

Apparently feeling the conversation needed to be shifted to a less intimate subject, Karen said, "Jade told me she runs the family drilling company because you opted out. I know you're an engineer—what didn't you like about drilling?"

"Everything," Zed answered. "The drilling itself is too mechanical and the office part is boring. I'm a graduate engineer because I didn't want to disappoint my grandfather, and I stayed with the company for the same reason until he died. But my bent isn't machines—it's animals and farming. I was meant to be a rancher in the same way Jade was born to drill wells. She loves what she calls the creativity of bringing water where it's needed, and she also dotes on every last old drilling rig in the yard, operative or not, insisting she'll get around to fixing them some day.''

"Awesome."

He nodded. "Her company's not the largest in the state, but Northern Nevada Drilling is widely respected. To date, Jade's brought in every well she's been hired to dig.''

Karen listened to him, admiring his respect for his sister's abilities, contrasting it to the way she sometimes felt about her half brother. Steve *was* successful in the sense that he made lots of money, but he never told her—or anyone—exactly what he was successful at. All she knew was he worked for the government. Their father thought he was the greatest thing on two feet.

The fact she was a successful, dedicated teacher didn't impress her dad at all. Her father seemed to equate success with money and, God knows, on a teacher's salary she'd never have much.

This was their father's problem, not hers or Steve's, but sometimes she had to remind herself not to resent her half brother.

"I really do love him," she said.

Looking startled, Zed asked, "Who?"

"I was thinking about Steve. He travels a lot—it's been ages since I've seen him." She glanced toward the bunk.

"It's not as easy as it used to be to pack up and go visiting."

"After yesterday, I can appreciate what you mean." He started to reach for her hand, hesitated and picked up the yellow toy duck instead. "Karen," he said, "we've got a problem, and I don't mean Danny."

Aware of exactly what he meant, she also knew there was no immediate solution. Covering her ears with her hands, she said, "No, don't tell me. I don't want to hear about any problem other than finding Danny's father."

Zed scowled. After a minute or two, still looking as dark as the sky outside, he began tossing the toy duck from hand to hand. She took her hands from her ears in time to hear him mutter something that sounded more like a hiss than a word, giving her an excuse to ask what he'd said.

He blinked as though coming out of a trance, glancing at her, then away. He set the duck carefully on the table. "I didn't realize I spoke aloud, and what I said isn't a real word, just syllables like Danny's babbling."

"Not a real word?" she repeated.

"I made it up as a child, or so Grandma told me. For some reason she hated to hear the word, so I learned to keep it to myself."

"Your private swearword?"

He shrugged. "I guess. But I wasn't swearing at you. This damn frustrating situation would make a saint swear." He waved his hand toward the cabin door. "To cap it off, the rain caused us to lose a day."

She reached across the table to touch his hand. "The day's not lost. The rain might delay us, but we didn't lose a day. Didn't we have an absolutely delicious broiled chicken picnic lunch, courtesy of The Colonel?''

He put his hand over hers, half-smiling. ''And great oatmeal chocolate chip cookies, courtesy of Karen Henderson.''

At that moment Danny let out a howl. ''Sound effects, courtesy of Daniel Shane Henderson,'' she added, rising to go to the bunk.

''Shane. Did Erin specify his middle name, too?''

''Yes, she did,'' Karen said. ''I've often wondered why she chose that middle name. The Danny is easy—her father's name is Daniel. It broke my heart that he never acknowledged what turned out to be her final attempt to gain his approval.''

''For what it's worth, my grandmother's maiden name was Shane,'' he said. ''A coincidence?''

''Since that blood match between you and Danny, I don't know if I believe in coincidence anymore. But if everything we've learned has significance, I sure don't understand what it is.''

Neither did he. He'd constructed a few theories, building them from fragments that might or might not prove to match, but the only fact he was perfectly sure of was that *he* wasn't Danny's father.

''I think I'll pass up the sail tomorrow,'' she said as she deftly changed the boy's wet diaper. ''But I'll come down to the marina later so we can cruise around and ask questions. What time do you think you'll be back?''

''Probably around one.''

With resignation he watched her reach for Danny's slicker. ''Here,'' she said when she had the boy cocooned. ''Take him while I get mine on.''

Zed hefted the boy in his arms, realizing how familiar it felt to hold him. Familiar and, somehow, right. "Bye, Tiger," he said.

Danny squirmed sideways and Zed realized he was trying to reach the duck on the table. He gave the toy to him. To his surprise, the boy promptly handed it back to him, saying, "Da!"

"He's honoring you with a gift," Karen said. "Be warned he may change his mind and demand the duck again a minute later."

"See you tomorrow, Tiger," Zed said as he handed Danny to Karen. "Thanks for the gift."

When she and the boy were gone, the boat cabin, cozy a moment before, seemed empty. He dealt with it by going out to eat.

George arrived promptly at seven the next morning, a beautiful morning with clear skies and a light breeze that promised good sailing. Zed eased the *Painted Lady* into the harbor and then through the channel to the ocean.

As usual when sailing, he forgot everything else for the time he was on the water, enjoying the quiet flight of a fine-tuned boat. Hours later they returned and, as he entered the channel, Zed's exhilaration began to fade.

"Good trip," George said. "Appreciate your patience with my crewing. I'm getting as slow as a desert tortoise."

"Hell, you're an old salt," Zed said. "What you lack in speed you more than make up for in knowledge. Never had a better crew. Let me know when we can go again."

On this sunshine day, all kinds of people strolled

around the waterfront. As Zed eased the boat into her mooring slip, a familiar voice hailed him.

"Zed!" Jade called. "It's about time you pulled in."

She leapt aboard as soon as he was close enough to the wharf and held out her hand to George, saying, "You must be Mr. Stone. I'm Zed's sister, Jade. Fantastic boat you've got here."

"Sorry you missed our sail," George said, smiling at her. Most men did. Jade's casual friendliness coupled with her good looks lent her an appealing charm.

"You must come with us next time," George added.

Jade thanked him and saw him off the boat while Zed battened down. When she returned, Karen and Danny were with her. "I parked them on a bench while we waited," Jade said.

Zed glanced at his watch. Not quite one.

"Jade saw the boat was gone, so she came by my apartment," Karen told him.

"Yeah, I heard the baby-sitting disaster story," Jade said, grinning. "A pink towel with purple flowers?"

Zed shrugged.

"And I met the famous Mrs. Hammond," Jade added. "I told her that while my brother actually was a certified nut, he would never dream of abducting a baby while naked."

He gave her a mock scowl. "Thanks a lot." Turning to Karen, he asked, "Do you want to come aboard?"

"First let's walk around till Danny gets tired," she responded.

"How about lunch?" he asked.

"Sounds good," Jade said. Karen nodded.

Zed shepherded them toward a small restaurant within

walking distance, recommended by George. When they neared the place, Zed saw George standing in front of the establishment talking to a man, a stranger.

"Oh, look, there's Mr. Stone," Jade said. "Let's invite him to lunch." Not waiting for anyone's agreement—one of her minor faults—she walked up and greeted him.

The man George was talking to turned at the sound of her voice, his gaze sliding over Jade to fix on Zed. "Speak of the devil, George," the stranger said. "That's him now."

He held out his hand to Zed. "Long time no see. Where the hell have you been keeping yourself, Talal?"

Chapter Seven

Zed stared blankly at the fiftyish man who'd called him Talal, the name echoing in his mind, growing louder and louder until it became a roaring in his ears. *Talal. Talal.* He'd never heard the name before and yet somewhere inside he knew that name. The tail end of a memory surfaced, something about sand and a ball, a red ball, but the memory slipped away before he could capture more, leaving him confused.

"I'm sorry," Jade said to the man, "but you've made a mistake. My brother isn't—"

"Wait," Zed told his sister. He offered his hand to the stranger. "My name's Zed Adams."

"Louie Quintas," the man said, shaking his hand.

"Louie's boat is moored four up from mine," George added. "I was just showing him the photo you gave me."

Louie scratched his head, looking from Zed to the photo

he still held, then back to Zed. "Guess you can't be Talal if you say you're not. But you sure could have fooled me. This is Talal in the picture, all right, on his boat. Talal Zohir. From one of those Middle Eastern oil countries—Kholi, as I recall."

"Kholi?" Zed echoed, his mind roiling in confusion. "Do you mind telling me how it is you know him?"

Louie glanced at George, who nodded. "Ran into him at a boat party a couple summers ago," Louie said. "We met again a week later when we were moored side by side at Catalina. You know how it is with us sailors, we don't stand on ceremony. My wife was with me and she got friendly with Talal's red-haired girlfriend." He pointed to Erin in the snapshot. "We shared a few margaritas while Talal and I swapped fish stories. You'd never know he was an Arab—didn't dress like one and spoke as good English as I do."

"This *is* the *Maddamti* you're talking about?" Zed asked.

Louie nodded. "Means 'my lady' in Arabic, Talal told me. My wife asked him if he'd named it for Erin."

"Had he?" Karen asked eagerly.

"He never did say one way or the other," Louie told her. "We took a lot of pictures in Catalina that year—some of him and the boat and Erin. My wife writes names, dates and places on the backs of all our photos to remind us where we were and when and who with. But Talal's name was so different I wouldn't have forgotten it, even without the reminder."

"Have you seen him since?" Jade asked, as usual getting right to the point. "Do you know where he is? We really do need to locate him. You might say it's a matter of life and death."

Zed, still feeling dazed since hearing the name Talal, let her assume control.

"Sorry, can't help you there," Louie said. "Never saw him again, never had an address. Happens a lot with sailors. Ships that pass in the night and all that."

"Have you ever heard his name mentioned since then?" Jade persisted.

Louie scratched his head again. "Come to think about it, in a way I did. Some guy, can't recall who, told me he'd heard somebody had seen my Arab friend's boat at Santa Barbara. *Maddamti*'s a name that tends to stand out."

"How long ago was this?" Jade asked.

"Maybe a week or more, can't pin it down."

"Only a week ago!" Karen exclaimed, her gaze meeting Zed's.

He couldn't seem to pull himself together. Though he'd asked questions and taken in everything that was said, it all had a dreamlike quality. Because of this, he couldn't match Karen's obvious excitement. What the devil was wrong with him?

"Didn't expect to hit a hole in one with my first shot," George said, laying a hand on Louie's arm. "Thanks, friend."

With her usual exuberant enthusiasm, Jade hugged Louie, saying, "You don't know how much we appreciate this."

Karen shifted Danny so she could shake Louie's hand. "Erin's my cousin," she said. "Thank you from the bottom of my heart for helping us."

Gathering his wits, Zed added, "I realize we can never repay you, but I can at least offer you lunch."

"Please do join us," Jade seconded.

Louie shook his head. "Nothing I'd like more, but I'm picking up my wife at her hairdresser in La Jolla and we're going on to a friend's house. Thanks for the offer. Glad I could help." He smiled at them, said, "See you, George," and walked briskly away.

For the past few minutes Zed had been half-aware that Danny was unhappy. He put aside his intention to invite George to lunch and asked Karen, "What's wrong with Tiger?"

"He's definitely not happy, that's for sure," she said. "He's been drooling a lot—probably he's cutting another tooth. I think I'd better take him home."

"Rain check for lunch?" Zed asked George. "I owe you."

"Don't sweat it," George told him. "Our sail this morning more than repaid me for everything. I do have one request, though. Once you find this Talal, please let me know how everything turns out."

Zed nodded. "Will do. If you'll come back to the boat, I'll return everything you gave me, because I intend to drive on up to Santa Barbara to check things out there."

Jade put a hand on his arm. "I'm going to take Karen and Danny back to her apartment," she said over Danny's whimpering. "See you there?"

He nodded, leaning down to peer into Danny's face. The boy sniffled, tears leaking from his eyes. He looked the picture of misery, and his discomfort hit Zed hard. "Hey, Tiger, I'd cut that tooth for you if I could," he said softly. "But it's in your mouth, so I can't. All I can do is feel sorry for you. Not much help, is it?'' He wiped a tear from Danny's cheek with his forefinger, straightened and said to Karen, "I'll come by as soon as I can."

By the time he'd neatened the boat's cabin, gathered his belongings and returned the keys to George, almost an hour had passed. As he and George walked to where their cars were parked, George said, "You seemed pretty well stunned by Louie's identification."

"I was. I never heard the name before and my acquaintance with any Arab is limited but..." His words trailed off and he shook his head. "I don't know why, but instead of being elated that we're on the way to finding the man in the picture, I feel apprehensive, as though something's wrong." He shrugged. "I guess I'll get over it."

At his car George clapped his hand on Zed's shoulder before sliding into the driver's seat. "Take it easy, sailor, and keep in touch," he said before closing the door and driving away.

No matter what Karen did, Danny refused to be comforted, making conversation with Jade difficult. Once home, Karen, with considerable difficulty, rubbed some of the pediatrician's recommended swollen-gum solution onto the reddened area of Danny's gums. She measured out a dose of baby pain reliever and coaxed it down him.

Danny wouldn't eat any solid food, finished only part of his bottle and wept piteously when Karen tried to lay him down. So she sat with him in the rocking chair until he finally dozed off and then put him down in his crib.

"Full-time job, isn't it?" Jade remarked when she dragged into the kitchen and flopped into a chair.

"And a half, sometimes," Karen admitted.

Jade slid a plate of food in front of her. "I slipped out to a deli for some goodies and made you a ham and cheese sandwich to go with the salads. I found your decaf and brewed a pot. Want some?"

"Thanks. At the moment I could use what Zed calls leaded coffee, but I'll stick with the decaf." She got up to pour herself a cup and returned to the table.

"Zed really flipped when Louie called him Talal—did you notice?" Jade asked.

Karen nodded. "He looked like he was in a trance for a few moments there."

"That's not like him. He even let me take over, he rarely lets me get away with that, though I try to do it a lot. I wonder if he'll tell us what was going through his head. He can be very private at times."

Karen nibbled on her thumbnail. She'd felt disappointed when Zed hadn't seemed to share her relief and excitement that they'd identified the man in the picture. Why hadn't he?

"He's certainly fallen for Danny in a big way," Jade said. "This is a guy who never paid the slightest attention to any of our friends' kids and yawned outright if anyone dared produce baby pictures in his presence. That little boy's a real charmer." Jade reached around to her bag, hung on the chair back, dug out an envelope and offered it to Karen. "Look inside, please."

Karen pulled out a snapshot and what looked to be a couple of picture proofs. Studying the baby in the photos, she frowned. "Why, these could be of Danny!" she exclaimed.

"They're of me, taken at six months," Jade said. "I thought there was a definite resemblance, more than just the generic one-baby-looks-like-another. Now you've confirmed it.''

"But I don't understand it," Karen admitted.

"Neither do I.''

"Did Zed run that half-brother possibility past you?" Karen asked. When Jade shook her head, Karen outlined what Zed had postulated. "He did point out the impossibility of finding the man if he did exist," she finished. "He said the difficulty is neither of you know anything about your father, not even his name.''

Jade sighed. "It's like we never had a father. Mother died when I was born, but we felt she was a part of our lives because our grandparents had so many pictures and spoke of her so often. I can't put much credence in this half-brother business, though. Not that I have a better idea. But I don't have to come up with any ideas, do I? We have a positive make on Talal Zohir—all that remains is to find him. I wish I could drive up to Santa Barbara with Zed, but I have to take an early flight on Monday so I can get back in time to bid on a drilling job that's a real biggie.''

"Don't worry. I've already decided to go with him. Danny and me, actually. I hate to take off more time, but this is critical. I want to be there when Zed confronts Talal. I have some choice words of my own to lay on that man.''

"I don't blame you. Go for it.''

Zed rang the bell and Karen let him in, hoping the sound hadn't roused Danny. When she didn't hear any noise from the bedroom, she returned to the kitchen, where Zed was heaping a plate with deli food.

"So Karen's going to Santa Barbara with you," Jade said to him.

Zed paused with a serving spoon in midair. "Not that I know of. I'm driving up there tonight." He looked at Karen. "Your school's in session—you told me you didn't want to take any more time off."

"I don't, but I can and I will," she told him.

"He may not be in Santa Barbara. I think it's best you stay here and let me try to locate him."

Karen raised her chin. "I'm going."

"What about Danny?" he asked.

"He's coming along. I don't travel without him."

"But he's sick. You can't haul along a sick baby."

She shook her head. "Cutting a tooth can't be classified as a major illness. He may be miserable, but he's not sick. The drive up to Santa Barbara won't hurt him—he tends to fall asleep in a car, so it might even help."

"You're as stubborn as they come." Exasperation tinged his words.

She raised an eyebrow. "How about tenacious? Or persistent? Or knows her own mind? Any one of those sounds better than stubborn. Besides, if I go, we can use my car and you can return the rental. I don't know how you feel about it, but I hate to waste money."

Zed turned to Jade. "I suppose you're on her side."

Jade nodded. "Women stick together whenever possible. Anyway, she's right—why waste money? Also, I have an ulterior motive. My plane doesn't leave till six tomorrow morning, so I'm spending the night here. If Karen goes with you, I get to sleep in her bed tonight instead of on her couch."

An hour and a half later Zed, Karen and a sleepy,

cranky Danny were on the road, heading north on Interstate 5. Zed was driving, and Karen was in the back with Danny. True to Karen's prediction, by the time they reached Oceanside the motion of the car had lulled the boy to sleep.

They were lucky enough not to hit any delays on the always crowded Los Angeles freeway system, making Zed's goal of a four-hour trip possible.

"How do you prune-pickers put up with this mess?" he asked Karen when they finally hit 101 and the traffic eased slightly.

"If prune-picker means a Californian, I'm not one," she replied tartly. "I'm a transplanted New Yorker. What do you call them—apple-pickers?"

"Never heard a name for New Yorkers," he admitted. "Too far away from Nevada, I guess. Carson's pretty close to the state line, so we see a lot of Californians coming and going and we like to pretend they're a bunch of weirdos."

"Some of them are," she admitted. "Like some New Yorkers. And probably Nevadans, too."

He grinned, glancing over his shoulder at her. "Present company excepted, I hope."

He caught her smile in the rearview mirror and his heart lifted. He preferred things easy between them, he was uncomfortable when they were at odds. If it wasn't for the chemistry between them, he and Karen could become good buddies. The problem was, you don't keep hoping you can get your good buddy into bed.

If she was beside him in the front seat, he'd be touching her—he couldn't seem to help it. She affected him in unexpected ways, even holding her hand could be erotic.

When he laid his hand over hers, she had a unique way of turning her hand so their palms met and then she'd caress his lightly but sensually. He could almost feel her fingers under his now. He took a deep breath and let it out slowly. Damn. Even with her in the back seat, he got aroused.

With Danny no longer needing her attention, Karen focused on Zed. No matter how she tried to set her mind on something else, her thoughts stubbornly clung to him. What would he do, she wondered, if she leaned forward and kissed his nape? If she licked his ear?

She'd probably cause an accident if she tried it, that's what would happen. Not that she'd actually do it—but she wanted to. And that was only the beginning of what she wanted. Fortunately she sat in the back and, with her seatbelt on, couldn't touch him if she tried.

Eventually, though, they'd stop for the night. And then? She shook her head. They'd be in different rooms; she'd insist on that. Anything else would be a mistake.

Danny woke up just outside Santa Barbara and set up such a howl that Zed pulled in to the first decent-looking motel he came to.

"Busy week with the horse show in town," the desk clerk said when Zed asked for two rooms. "Nothing left but a suite."

Remembering Danny's plaintive crying, Zed had no heart to get back into the car and look for another place. He took the suite and asked for a crib to be placed in it.

He explained the situation to Karen as he drove around to the back of the motel. "Anything," she said as she tried without success to comfort Danny. "Just as long as we don't have to share a bed."

"Sharing a bed isn't a plus?" he teased.

Without replying, she slanted him a speaking look.

They discovered the two rooms of the suite were separated by an archway rather than a door, with two double beds in one and a queen-size in the other. There was only one bath, large, with a whirlpool tub in addition to the shower.

"I didn't think to bring a swimsuit," Karen said regretfully.

Zed shrugged. "There's always underwear. Why don't you strip Tiger while I fill the tub, and I'll take him in with me? Maybe that'll distract him."

"I'm willing to try anything at this point," she said. "Just don't get the water too hot."

At first the boy eyed the seething water with suspicion and he clung to Karen, refusing to go to Zed. Soon he stopped crying, obviously fascinated by the bubbling. Zed began whistling, choosing a country-western song. This one, as he recalled, dealt with unrequited love in El Paso.

Finally Danny reached out to him and he took the boy from Karen, easing him down slowly onto his knee, watching as Danny's expression changed from dubious to interested. Moments later he was slapping his hand against the bubbling water. Holding the little naked body next to him gave Zed an overwhelming feeling of protectiveness. By God, no one was ever going to hurt this kid, not as long as he was around.

Intent on the boy, he didn't realize Karen had disappeared until she returned, wearing a short terry-cloth robe.

"Don't look," she warned. "You'll make me self-conscious."

"I hope you realize the first reaction to being told not to look is to stare," he told her.

"I'm not coming in unless you look away."

He complied, heard her step into the tub, gave her a moment to seat herself and then turned toward her again. Only her head and shoulders rose above the water. He could see straps over her shoulders, so he knew she must be wearing a bra and panties, just as he was wearing his boxer shorts. His loins tightened as he pictured her stepping out of the tub with the wet bra and panties molded to her body, the next best thing to being naked.

"Tiger isn't at all modest," he said. "To him being naked is perfectly natural. Too bad we have to grow up and change. I'm partial to nakedness myself."

Karen rolled her eyes. "Tell me."

"I'd go naked more often if the world wasn't filled with Mrs. Hammonds."

Karen hadn't seen him in the towel, but she vividly recalled his penchant for wearing sweatpants that hung precariously on his hips, so low it was evident he wore nothing beneath them. She also remembered how she'd anticipated their fall. She knew he'd left his shorts on before climbing into the tub, because she'd watched him from the corner of her eye while she was stripping Danny.

And, of course, there'd been that one time at the ranch when he'd rushed out of his bedroom without any clothes on. Unfortunately, she'd been too occupied with Danny to pay close attention. At the moment, she was very aware of his near nakedness so close to her. Water beaded his black chest hair, the beads breaking and trickling down.

When she realized her gaze was following each tiny rivulet, she forced herself to stop and look at Danny instead. Noting the contrast of Danny's lighter skin against Zed's tanned arms and torso made her try to remember if Zed's tan extended below his waist. She couldn't recall seeing a demarcation line when he was wearing those low-slung sweats.

"I need a shave," he said, evidently conscious of her scrutiny. He rubbed a hand over his dark stubble. "Didn't get around to it this morning."

No way was she going to admit she found his unshaven look sexy. Nor that she admired the play of his shoulder muscles when he moved his arms. "The moisture's making your hair curl tighter," she said. "It does the same thing to Danny's."

Zed wound one of Danny's brown curls around his forefinger. The boy turned to glance at him and stuck a finger between Zed's lips.

"I guess that means whistle. Let's let Karen pick the tune. What's your pleasure, my lady?"

A frisson ran along her spine at the "my lady," even though she knew it was merely a meaningless phrase. When she'd been in his arms the other night he'd called her "my beautiful Karen." Quite likely that had no meaning, either, beyond the passing moment, but she still cherished the words.

"You must be influenced by the *Maddamti*," she said. "If we're getting into things Arabic, how about a real oldie, 'The Sheik of Araby'?"

"I'll give it a whirl." As soon as he began to whistle, Danny started to rock back and forth in time to the beat.

Karen smiled, a surge of happiness lapping through her.

If only it could always be this way, she and Danny and Zed.... She took a deep breath and let it out slowly, her smile fading as she reminded herself of their purpose in coming to Santa Barbara. With luck, tomorrow they'd find the *Maddamti* moored in the harbor and their search for Danny's father would be over.

Why wasn't she more exhilarated at the possibility? Her aim from the moment Danny was born had been to locate his father. Now she was on the verge of accomplishing that. But then what? Zed would have no reason to stick around; he'd be off to Nevada. Would she ever see him again?

"Do you think we'll actually find him?" she asked.

Zed shrugged. He stopped whistling, at the same time lifting Danny off his knee and bouncing him up and down in the bubbling water. "If the boat's here, our chances are excellent. Even if he's merely moored it here for the time being, they'll have an address. If the boat's not here, someone may know where he was headed."

He sounded more enthusiastic than she felt. But why not? He'd been put through a lot of turmoil because of Talal Zohir. Part of it had been her fault, hers and Joe Santoro's, but that couldn't be helped. After this disruption of his life, Zed probably couldn't wait to get things settled and go home.

Danny laughed aloud, riveting her attention. "You're a regular water baby," she told him. He squealed with delight and held out his arms to her.

Zed relinquished the boy to Karen, watching how lovingly she nuzzled Danny's neck as she hugged him to her. Had she, he wondered, thought of what might happen once they located the boy's father? Would Talal Zohir accept his responsibility? And, if he did, how would he do it? Would he pay support for the boy, allowing Karen to keep Danny, or would he decide to raise his son himself?

Karen would be devastated to lose Danny. The boy would be unhappy as well, but kids were resilient and he'd come to accept a new life, while Karen would mourn his loss for years, maybe all her life. He didn't want to see that happen. Yet they were too close to turn back. Not only did Danny deserve a father but he, himself, was eager to confront this man who looked so much like him that he'd complicated Zed's life.

Karen lifted a red ball from the edge of the tub and floated it on the water toward Danny, who reached for the ball, almost flinging himself from her arms. A sense of *déjà vu* crept over Zed as he watched. A child, a red ball—it seemed so familiar. Familiar and yet wrong. This was water when it should be sand....

"Gone into another trance?" Karen asked, making him blink.

"Another trance?" he echoed.

"Like the one earlier today. Both Jade and I noticed how you spaced out when Louie called you Talal."

He couldn't bring himself to talk about what he'd felt. It wasn't that he minded if she thought him weird, but his feelings then and now were too nebulous and private to be put into words. "Stunned the first time, sleepy the second," he told her, which was a partial truth.

"Sleepy means it's time to get out of the tub before we get too much of a good thing." Hefting Danny, she started to climb out, then hesitated.

Aware she was waiting for him to go ahead of her, he

said, "Ladies and children first. That's an old shipboard rule."

"We're not aboard ship." Though she spoke tartly, she proceeded to climb from the tub.

As he'd anticipated, her wet, silky underwear clung to her, revealing a sweetly rounded bottom. Unfortunately, Danny's body effectively concealed her breasts but, he told himself, it was just as well, since he was already turned on to the point of discomfort.

When she vanished into the room she'd chosen, he eased out, took off his shorts, wrung the water from them and pulled the tub plug. He padded naked into his room, towel-dried himself and then grabbed his jeans. First they'd eat, Danny would fall asleep and then what?

Go to bed? Probably, though not necessarily in the way he'd choose. She'd be in her room in her bed and he'd be in his room in his bed. Unless he could change her mind. He was off the hook now. Karen knew he wasn't Danny's father, so there was no reason he shouldn't make love to her. But that didn't mean she intended to cooperate.

He didn't recall ever wanting a woman as much as he wanted Karen. She was so beautiful, she fit into his arms so perfectly and her eager response to him was erotic nectar, making him drunk with desire.

He imagined her in his bed, naked, no clothes hampering their enjoyment of each other. He'd make slow, sweet love to her, make it last.... He shook his head. This was no way to get turned off.

Ordinarily, after a long day that began at 5:00 a.m. as this one had, he could be sure of dropping into bed and being asleep before he hit the pillow. He didn't think that would work under the present circumstances. In fact, he suspected he was going to find the night even longer than the day had been.

MAX FOOLED
he did work without the on-
understood he was going to...
he did work without the on-

Chapter Eight

After dinner Karen breathed a sigh of relief when Danny accepted the motel crib without protest, closing his eyes and falling asleep almost immediately. Now that the troublesome tooth had poked through the gum, he was no longer in pain, thank heaven. For the moment she had no worries about him.

She wished she could say the same for herself. What was she going to do? The coward's way would be to undress and crawl into bed without leaving the room, avoiding any chance of encountering Zed. She wasn't a coward. What was she, then? A woman who didn't know her own mind? Or one who knew her own mind but was afraid to acknowledge that she did?

Whatever, she was so bemused by Zed Adams that she couldn't be in the same room he was in without wanting to touch him, aware that a touch might lead to a kiss and a kiss would lead to her wanting more and more and more. And after that, where would she be?

Though she hadn't accused him, she was sure he'd taken off his shorts on purpose after leaving the tub, knowing very well she'd watch him go into his room. The glimpse she'd gotten had been from the rear, hinting without revealing, a real teaser.

Now that they'd discovered the man in the photo was not Zed, there was no real reason they couldn't make love. Obviously he wanted to. So did she. Why did she hesitate? Was she waiting for some kind of a commitment when she had no reason to expect any?

"Stop dithering," she muttered. "Say good-night to the man and go to bed. Alone."

"Danny okay?" Zed called from the other room.

Karen straightened her shoulders, ran a hand through her hair and walked through the archway, prepared to tell him Danny was asleep and that she soon would be. Zed, she noted, had changed from the jeans and T-shirt he'd worn to go out and bring back pizza. He was back in those damn low-slung sweatpants and no shirt, distracting her.

She marched across to where he stood in the tiny neutral territory between the rooms, yanked up his pants and said, "I'll hold them in place while you retie the waist cord."

"I don't recall ever getting an offer quite like that," he said.

"I suppose everyone else wants to see them fall off," she snapped. "*I* don't." Even as she spoke, she realized it was a big mistake to get this close to him. He'd shaved, so a spicy after-shave scent mingled with his own intriguing musk.

Her fingers, holding the waistband, were pressed against his warm, bare flesh, the contact sending urgent messages along her nerves that translated to yes, yes, we want more.

"You smell delicious," he murmured as he fumbled with the cord. "Good enough to kiss." Without touching her otherwise, he leaned and brushed his lips over hers. "You taste even better," he said, easing away enough to gaze into her eyes.

Determined not to fall into the darkness of his eyes and lose all contact with reality, she closed hers. "Tie the damn cord," she said. Instead of the no-nonsense tone she tried for, her words came out in a husky whisper.

Realizing she couldn't resist her own need much longer, she opened her eyes, at the same time releasing the waistband of his sweatpants and stepping back.

"Whoa!" he exclaimed, grabbing at the pants barely in time.

"Good night, Zed," she said hastily, and fled into her bedroom with the taste of him still on her lips and the need for him heating her body.

"So I'm a coward," she muttered as she got ready for bed. "I'm just not ready to handle how I feel about him."

For a person who had always been in charge, it was scary to lose control; she was too afraid of the consequences. Erin hadn't worried about consequences and Erin was dead. Not that Karen feared getting pregnant—she knew better. Losing control was another matter. It meant that she'd be giving in to an emotion that scared her because of its intensity.

She'd never once felt for any other man what she did for Zed—an overwhelming, aching need that demanded fulfillment. Worse, she feared another emotion was becoming linked with the physical attraction, one she was almost afraid to name.

With her responsibility for Danny to think about, she couldn't afford to fall in love. She leaned over the crib to check on him, covering his rump, sticking up as usual, with the blanket. Danny must always come first.

After brushing her teeth, she slid into bed. As she closed her eyes, seeking sleep, the aftertaste of mint faded from her mouth, replaced by the memory of Zed's dark, enticing taste. He was, it seemed, going to spend the night with her one way or another.

Though he hadn't expected to, Zed fell asleep almost instantly, only to rouse two hours later to Danny's wail. He sprang up and started for the other room, hesitated, then grabbed his sweatpants and yanked them on. In her bedroom he found Karen sitting on the bed with Danny on her lap.

"What's wrong?" he asked, sitting next to her and touching Danny's forehead gently. "He doesn't feel hot."

"I'm not sure," she said. "I don't think he's sick. My guess is he bit down on that new tooth in his sleep and the gum is still sensitive. If you'll hand me that zipper bag from the dresser I'll rub some stuff on his gums."

Danny didn't want anything rubbed on his gums and refused to open his mouth. Nor would he swallow the baby pain reliever she tried to give him. He took a couple of sucks on the bottle nipple and turned his head away, emitting another wail.

"Okay, Tiger, time to have this out man to man," Zed said. He picked up the boy, positioned him against his chest, held him there and began pacing through the two rooms, in and out and in and out, whistling as he walked. Danny's crying gradually subsided. When Zed felt him relax under his hands, he stopped whistling but kept walking, slowing his pace.

Karen came alongside him to peer at Danny. "He's asleep," she whispered.

But when Zed tried to put him back into the crib, Danny clung to him. Sighing, Zed eased down onto Karen's bed, stretching out and shifting the boy so Danny lay on his chest. Karen spread a baby blanket over him, then curled next to Zed, pulling up the covers.

For a time Zed was afraid to speak for fear of waking Danny, but when he realized that Karen was laughing, he whispered, "What's so funny?"

"Did you realize what you were whistling?" she asked softly.

"Not really."

"It took me a while to place the song. I'm into old movies and I think it's from a Fred Astaire film, though I believe I've heard a Sinatra version. I'm not sure of the song's actual name, but it says something about one for my baby and one for the road."

Zed smiled, amused at what his subconscious had come up with.

"He's attuned to your heartbeat now," she said.

"My heartbeat?"

"That's what he hears when he lies against your chest. The beat is reassuring and makes him relax. Don't forget that before he's born a baby listens to his mother's heartbeat for nine months."

Zed lay there marveling that the beating of his heart

could reassure Danny enough to put the boy to sleep. Though he was acutely aware of Karen next to him, his desire for her was mixed with contentment. The three of them were together and, for the moment, that was enough.

The last thing he intended to do was to fall asleep....

After wandering alone and confused in a concealing mist for what seemed like forever, he grew aware that he was rising off the ground, floating in a pleasant warmth, no longer alone. Karen floated with him in a soft nimbus, her fingers lightly stroking his lips, gently caressing his face, touching his closed eyelids....

Zed woke abruptly to a room light with morning and Danny peering into his face. "Da," Danny said as Zed removed the boy's finger from his nose. "Da, da."

Next to them, Karen groaned and turned over so she faced in their direction. "It's morning!" she cried. "I must have fallen asleep."

"We shared a bed after all," Zed told her.

After breakfast they drove to the marina and talked to the woman who registered the boats. "Yeah, I remember the *Maddamti*," she said. "Hard to forget a name like that. The boat's not here, though. Her owner sailed north yesterday, heading for Monterey. We warned him a storm was edging down the coast, but he figured he could make it around the peninsula and into Monterey Bay before the front reached San Francisco."

Remembering the weather map he'd watched on TV this morning, Zed shook his head. "I wouldn't care to try it."

"If he has any sense he'll put in at Carmel," the woman said. "This northern coast is trickier than sailors who aren't from around here realize.'' She narrowed her eyes at Zed. ''You know, if you had a beard you'd look a lot like that guy.''

Zed half smiled. ''So I've been told. Thanks for your info.''

As they left, Zed said to Karen, ''Missed him by a day. Maybe the Paiutes have something with their idea of a trickster somewhere out there interfering with us.''

Karen shrugged. ''We know where he's headed and that he's grown a beard. The only question is Carmel or Monterey?''

''We can stop in Carmel and check but I'd bet this guy's going to chance the peninsula and go all the way. He's a risk taker. I feel it in my bones.''

They made good time as they traveled north on Highway 1. If Zed hadn't been so intent on catching up with *Maddamti*'s owner, he could have relaxed and enjoyed the spectacular beauty of the rugged coastline but, as it was, he felt driven. Outside Carmel the clouds that had been gathering and thickening rose to cover the sky.

''He's a damn fool if he didn't pull in to Carmel Bay,'' Zed told Karen.

But, as they discovered at the marina, the *Maddamti* was not moored in the bay. A thin, wind-driven rain began before they got back to the car. ''From here we cut across the peninsula,'' he said. ''By car it's only a few miles. By boat it's a long way around and no place to be in a storm. Let's hope he's made it already.''

Visibility on Highway 1 soon dropped from poor to miserable, and the wipers were unable to keep up with the sheets of rain drenching the peninsula. Blasts of wind forced Zed to clench his hands on the wheel to keep the car on the road.

"Maybe *we* should have stayed in Carmel," Karen said.

He glanced back at her, noting that Danny had fallen asleep in his car seat, undisturbed by the violence of the storm. "It's not far," he told her. "Less than ten miles—we'll make it."

The lack of visibility forced Zed to reduce speed until the car was barely crawling along, headlights next to useless in the heavy rain. A van blasted by him, cutting in ahead of him with inches to spare, leaving him muttering curses under his breath at the driver's stupidity. He rounded a curve and sucked in his breath in dread. Directly ahead of him the van slanted crosswise in his lane, the needled branches of a fallen fir looming above the wrecked car.

With a rocky bank to his right, the van directly ahead and the downed tree blocking the left lane, there was no escape. "Hang on!" he called to Karen as he fought to bring the car to a halt without slamming into any of the obstacles.

For a split second he thought he might make it, then the tires skidded on the wet pavement. He struggled for control, but with a sickening screech of torn metal the rear left side of the car rammed the back of the van. The driver's air bag deployed, cutting off Zed's vision. Karen's screams echoed in his ears and the insidious odor of gasoline filled his nostrils.

Unable to get out the driver's side, Zed fought his way free of the air bag, flung himself through the opposite door, wrenched open the back door on that side and dived inside, calling Karen's name. "Are you hurt?" he asked.

"Please help me," she begged, her voice quivering. "I can't seem to get Danny out of his car seat."

The van's headlights shed enough illumination for Zed to see why. The boy was pinned by a chunk of metal that curved into the car seat. Rather than risking injury to Danny by trying to lift him from the seat, Zed eased the protesting Karen out of the car and then struggled to unlatch the car seat itself.

"It's okay, Tiger," he muttered as he worked, "I'll get you out of here, don't worry. Everything's going to be all right." He refused to let himself believe otherwise; he wouldn't let himself wonder why the boy wasn't crying.

He finally wriggled the seat loose and away from the bulging metal. As he hoisted Danny, seat and all, from the wrecked car into the rain, he heard the wail of an approaching emergency vehicle and prayed it was an ambulance.

Karen couldn't remember exactly how she and Zed had gotten to the emergency waiting room of the hospital. Had they ridden in the ambulance with Danny? She clung to Zed's hand, her dazed mind filled with apprehension. Miraculously, both she and Zed had escaped serious injury but, if she could, she'd gladly trade places with Danny, who had been hurt. No one had yet told her how badly. All she knew was that he'd been unconscious when they took him off to be X-rayed. At the moment she and Zed were waiting for the doctors to finish a CAT scan.

Zed put his arm around her and she rested her head on his shoulder, as comforted as she could feel under the circumstances. "He's going to be all right," she whispered.

"Believe it," he assured her.

The door to the emergency treatment area opened and a nurse motioned to them. When they hurried to her, she drew them inside and said, "Danny may need blood. The problem is he has an unusual type—"

Zed interrupted. "My blood matches his. I can donate blood for him."

The nurse—Penny Norton, according to her badge—frowned. "Are you certain?"

Zed nodded and Karen said, "Yes, it's true. Zed's and Danny's blood matches all the way. How is Danny? Can I see him?"

"In a few minutes," the nurse said. "We'll let you know. If you'll come with me, Zed, we'll test your blood."

Reluctant to be parted from Zed for even a moment, Karen accompanied him into a cubicle, where he lay on a stretcherlike table. A technician wearing gloves and a mask drew blood from him and took the sample away.

Whether it was minutes or hours later that she came back Karen couldn't be sure. Time had no meaning, no reality. Penny and the technician set up equipment and put a needle into Zed's arm. Soon Karen could see his blood filling a plastic container. At that point one of the doctors poked his head into the cubicle. "Karen Henderson?" he asked.

Karen left Zed to join the doctor, who shook her hand. "Dr. Nelson," he said. "I'm a neurosurgeon. I've looked at your son's pictures and we may have to operate to relieve a hematoma." He sat her down at a desk and drew her a picture, explaining how a blood clot had formed inside Danny's skull due to his head being banged against the metal.

"The clot can cause pressure against the brain, which is dangerous. If it gets any larger we'll have to intervene to prevent brain damage."

Karen swallowed. "What if it doesn't get any bigger?"

Dr. Nelson smiled. "We can always hope the clot will resolve and be absorbed instead. In which case, surgery may not be needed."

"Is there—" Her voice faltered and she had to clear her throat before she could go on. "Does he have any other injuries?"

"A few scrapes and bruises. Nothing to worry you or us. We've admitted him to ICU—undoubtedly you'd like to be with him. I'll have you sign the necessary forms there."

At the sight of Danny lying in a rolling bed with tubes stuck into him, Karen took a deep breath and let it out while she counted to ten. No matter how tiny and helpless he looked, this was not the time to cry. She sat on the stool next to the bed and put her hand to his cheek. "I'm here, sweetie," she murmured. "Karen's here. I won't leave you, I won't ever leave you."

It broke her heart to realize she couldn't promise to keep him safe, nor could she assure him everything was all right. Blinking back tears, she very gently began to stroke his legs and arms, careful to avoid the tubes. Not once did she glance up at what she knew must be the monitors showing his heartbeats. He was alive and she was with him—that's all she could be sure of right now.

* * *

Zed, sitting impatiently on the edge of the table after his blood had been drawn, said to Penny, "I feel fine. Not at all dizzy. There's no need to keep me here."

"You're the judge," she said. "But take it easy for a few minutes, okay?"

He slid off the table. "Can you tell me where Karen and Danny are?"

"The boy's in ICU and I imagine she's with him." Penny told him how to get there.

Like all hospitals, this one had too many twisty corridors where a guy could get lost, but he finally came to a door with an ICU label. As he pushed it open, a nurse appeared. "Who are you visiting?" she asked. "Are you a relative?" Before he answered, she shook her head. "I don't know why I bothered to ask. Of course you're a relative—you look just like him. He's in 5A." She gestured to her left. "Around that way."

Zed hurried in that direction, finding 5A with no difficulty, a cubicle with no door rather than a room. He entered and stopped short, staring. Not at Danny but at the man who lay in the bed, obviously unconscious. He was dark haired, with a curly black beard. Despite the beard, Zed immediately recognized him as the man in the photo. The man he was searching for.

He'd known all along there was a marked resemblance between him and the man in the photo, but that hadn't prepared him for seeing the man in the flesh. He advanced slowly toward the bed.

"Sir?" The voice came from behind him. Zed turned to see the nurse who'd directed him here. "If you don't mind, Dr. Nelson would like to speak to you. He's waiting at the desk."

Unsure what to do, Zed followed her to the nursing station. A tall blond man rose from his chair and shook his hand, saying, "Dr. Nelson. You're Zed Adams?"

Zed nodded.

"I know you came in with Danny Henderson. Are you related to the man in 5A?"

Zed hesitated. Was he? Didn't he have to be, considering everything? "No, I'm not," he said finally. "There was a misunderstanding and the nurse misdirected me here—I was looking for Danny's room."

"I've encouraging news for you about Danny," the doctor said. "The clot hasn't grown larger, his vital signs are improving, and he's beginning to respond. Unless his condition changes radically, it doesn't look as though Danny will need the surgery you donated blood for."

Zed's heart leapt. "That's the best news I've ever heard."

Dr. Nelson nodded. "The man in 5A is another matter. He's lost a lot of blood from his injuries—a compound fracture of his left tibia and a shattered ankle. He'd be in surgery now except for the fact they didn't have a blood match for him. At least, not until you appeared."

Zed stared at him. "What do I have to do with it?"

"Your blood is a perfect match. Both of you have this rare component—"

"A match to Danny's blood, you mean."

"That, too. The lab tech couldn't believe her eyes when she was sent three samples in a row and they all matched down to the last component. She mentioned this remarkable coincidence to me and I told the orthopedic surgeon I'd talk to you. What I'm saying is that the blood you donated for Danny is needed for the man in 5A. It's really an emergency."

Zed frowned. "But what if Danny needs the blood?"

"I doubt he will. If I'm wrong, well, we didn't exactly drain you, you know. You can spare another pint, should it become necessary."

"Go ahead, then. Glad to help."

Dr. Nelson nodded. "Thanks."

"Can you tell me what kind of an accident caused the man's injuries?"

"I heard his sailboat rammed rocks outside the harbor in the storm. He was lucky to be rescued before he drowned or bled to death." He pointed to a room directly across from the station. "Danny's in there."

Zed found Karen seated beside Danny's bed. She turned to him. "He's better," she said with a smile. "I'm so relieved. They may move him to the pediatric ward, where he can be in a crib."

Gazing down at Danny, Zed felt his heart contract. Dark bruises discolored the boy's face and he lay so still in the bed. Too still. "Are you sure he's better?" he blurted.

"Dr. Nelson told me so. Besides, Danny's moved his arms and made sucking sounds like he's coming out of his coma. I think he's searching for his blue horse. We'll have to find it."

Zed nodded. He meant to tell her about the man in 5A. He had to be Talal Zohir, though Zed had deliberately not asked the man's name because, somehow, he was reluctant to hear it. He wanted to talk to Karen about all this, but found he couldn't. Not yet. Not until he understood what the blood match meant. Despite his apprehension over Danny, he had to fight an urge to return to 5A even though he couldn't possibly learn any more from an unconscious man than he already knew.

Why had the memory of the red ball and the sand flashed through his mind when he looked at the bearded man's face? It was as if he groped through a mist as dense as the fog in his dreams. None of it made any sense.

Chapter Nine

Close to midnight the doctor decided Danny's condition had stabilized and he could be moved to pediatrics. Since Karen would be with the boy, Zed realized he could be spared for a while. Karen had insisted she wasn't hungry, but he planned to bring back some food if he could locate any. Also, he needed to find out from the police where Karen's car had been towed so they could retrieve their belongings in the morning.

After talking to the police from a pay phone in the hospital lobby, he called a cab. When it arrived, he hurried out, noticing in passing that no more than a drizzle remained of the rain.

"Food?" the cabbie said when Zed asked him. "Getting pretty late. Your best bet's got to be this supermarket that stays open twenty-four hours. You want I should take you there?"

"Yeah. And wait for me."

In the market the deli was closed, so Zed foraged along the shelves, emerging from the market with crackers, cheese, peanut butter, plastic knives, soft drinks and, just in case, arrowroot biscuits. His prize, though, was the blue octopus stuffed toy he'd spotted on his way to the check-out counter. Maybe Danny wouldn't accept a tentacle in place of his horse's ear, but it was worth a try. At least it was blue, if that meant anything.

He paid off the cab and reentered the hospital. He'd been told where pediatrics was but, instead, he found himself returning to ICU.

"Has Talal Zohir been to surgery yet?" he asked the nurse on duty.

"He's still in the operating room," she replied.

He started to ask her how Talal was doing but stopped himself as he realized she'd have no way to know. "Thanks," he said and left ICU.

On the next floor he located Danny's room and brought in his booty to share with Karen. Despite the dark circles under her eyes, she smiled when she saw the toy he'd bought.

"A blue octopus, of all things," she said, shaking her head.

"How is he?"

"When they moved him, he opened his eyes and looked at me. The nurse said that was a good sign."

As if summoned by Karen's words, a nurse entered the room. She checked on Danny, then motioned to them to move away from the crib toward the door.

"Look," she said, "you both need sleep. We don't have any facilities here for parents, but there's a bed-and-breakfast two blocks away. I've sent people there before, and they've reported that the place was very nice.''

"I don't want to leave Danny," Karen protested.

"I understand. But if you don't sleep, when he does wake up fully, rather than the rested mom and dad he needs, he'll get two frazzled parents.''

"What if he wakes up and I'm not here?" Karen said. "He'll be frightened.''

"He's not going to be fully awake until a lot later this morning. What he'll do is drift in and out of consciousness for a while—he won't be aware enough to miss you. In the long run, you'll be doing him as well as yourselves a favor by catching a few hours of sleep. After all, as I understand it, you were involved in the accident, too. That takes its toll.''

Karen began chewing on her thumbnail. "I don't know," she said.

"What's the name of this place?" Zed asked. "And will they take us at this late hour?''

The nurse nodded. "They're used to hospital referrals.'' She gave him the name and phone number, adding, "I'll call them for you if you like.''

Without discussing it with Karen, he nodded. "Two,'' he said to the nurse.

She exited, returning a few minutes later. "The lady at Snug Haven said you can come right over. She'll have everything ready by the time you get there.''

Karen looked at him, frowning. He put his hands on her shoulders. "You're too tired to think straight,'' he told her, "and I'm not much better. We're taking the nurse's recommendation.''

Despite her obvious uncertainty, Zed shepherded Karen

from the room, stopping at the nurses' station to make certain they'd call to notify them if there was any change in Danny's condition.

They walked the two blocks to the bed-and-breakfast in the cool night mist, Karen clinging to his arm as though she were too exhausted to make it on her own. "Snug Haven," she murmured, reading the sign posted on the lawn in front of a Victorian-era house.

An older woman with graying braids down her back and wearing a long green robe led them up the stairs and into a large room. "Here you are," she said. "We can settle up later this morning." She was gone before Zed took in the fact that there was only the one room, not a suite. Furthermore, there was just one place to sleep in the room, a brass bed—a double, if he wasn't mistaken.

"I asked for two," he said to Karen, somewhat unsure whether he'd specified two rooms or two beds. "You take this one and I'll—"

She clutched his arm. "No," she said, "don't leave me. I couldn't bear to be alone."

He didn't much fancy being alone, either, but, even as exhausted as he felt, he knew sleeping in the same bed with Karen without making love to her would be a real challenge. Spotting an afghan thrown over a chair, he said, "I'll sleep on top of the covers and use the afghan."

With all their belongings still in the car, unreachable until the garage opened later in the day, they had no reason to undress. Her shoes off, Karen padded into the bathroom first. Zed kicked off his shoes and removed his shirt while he waited for his turn. When he came out of the bathroom, Karen was already curled into a ball under the bed covers, sound asleep. He grabbed the afghan in passing and flopped on top of the bed.

Karen woke to darkness with no idea where she was. Groggy with sleep, she tried to orient herself. Not home. A motel? But motels usually didn't smell of potpourri. So where on earth was she? Throwing the covers back, she started to sit up to grope for a bedside lamp. Then, suddenly, she realized she wasn't alone in the bed.

"What's wrong?" a man's voice asked, sleepily slurring the words. She recognized the voice as Zed's and everything flooded back—the drive north, the accident, Danny....

She reached for Zed, seeking reassurance and comfort. "Oh, Zed," she cried, "do you think he's all right?"

He shifted position, gathering her into his arms and pulling her down next to him. "Shh, don't worry. If anything had gone wrong, we'd have been notified. You know he was improving when we left."

Zed's hand stroked her back, warm through her shirt. She buried her face in his shoulder, comforted by his familiar smell and his solid presence. "Close your eyes and relax," he murmured. "The worst is over. No more bad things are going to happen."

The assurance in his voice made her believe him. Danny *was* improving, the nurse had said so and she had seen for herself that he was better. Snuggling closer, she whispered, "I'm glad you're here with me."

"I am, too. This is no time to be alone."

She closed her eyes, knowing she was safe in his arms. "Snug haven," she murmured drowsily, sinking back into sleep's embrace.

Sleep eluded Zed. Holding Karen close kept him aroused, despite his effort to detach himself from his erotic feelings. He wanted her—he couldn't help himself—but he was determined not to act on his need. At least, not here and now. When she finally sighed and turned away from him in her sleep, he breathed a sigh of relief and eased quietly from the bed. A look at his watch told him it was a few minutes past five-thirty. He groped for his shirt and his shoes, found them and let himself out of the room.

He padded carefully down the stairs, donning his shirt and shoes before letting himself out into the still-dark morning.

At the hospital he checked on Danny, who was either sleeping or still unconscious. "Sleeping," the nurse said when he asked. "He woke all the way up, looked around and seemed about to cry. I handed him that stuffed toy you left in his crib. He clutched it to him and closed his eyes again."

Reassured, Zed sat by Danny's crib for a while in case the boy roused again. After a time he decided Danny wasn't going to wake up and therefore didn't need him. He left pediatrics, intending to have some coffee before returning to Snug Haven but, instead of heading for the coffee machine in the lobby, he found himself outside ICU.

When he pushed open the door the nurse smiled at him. "Talal's relative, right? He's come back from the recovery room and his vitals are stable. You can go in and see him, if you like."

Zed hesitated, then turned toward 5A. He walked slowly up to Talal's bed and gazed down at him. He was still out for the count, with tubes stuck everywhere and his left leg in a cast that was propped on pillows. Zed was about to turn away when, to his surprise, Talal's eyelids fluttered and opened. Dark eyes stared into his. *"Zeid?"* Talal whispered.

A shock wave shook through Zed, penetrating to the marrow of his bones. Though the word sounded strange with Talal's pronunciation, he'd spoken Zed's name.

How in hell can he possibly know who I am? Zed asked himself.

Talal's eyes closed and he began breathing deeply again, leaving Zed confused and mystified, aware Talal was in no condition to answer the questions roiling in his mind.

Coffee forgotten, he returned to Snug Haven. As he opened the door the enticing smell of food cooking made his stomach gurgle. The bed-and-breakfast owner appeared at the end of the hall, wearing a blue knit dress, her braids neatly coiled around her head. "Up so soon?" she asked. "Breakfast won't be ready for a half hour."

"Is it possible I could have a cup of coffee while I wait?" he asked.

"Of course. Cream and sugar?"

"Just a tad of each."

When she returned with a man-size mug of coffee, he thanked her and carried it upstairs. Karen was still huddled under the covers. He tried to be quiet, but she roused when he entered. "I've been to see Danny," he told her. "He's doing fine, actually sleeping instead of being in a coma."

He held back the fact that he'd stopped to visit Talal, not quite ready to share the strange response he'd gotten.

"I've been informed breakfast will be served in a half hour," he added.

"Thank heaven—I'm starved. You're sure Danny's okay?"

"Confirmed by the nurse."

She eased from the bed, running a hand through her hair. "I wish I didn't feel so grungy."

She might feel grungy, but he thought she looked as sexy as hell with her hair tousled and that sleepy daze in her eyes. "I'll retrieve our belongings after breakfast," he said, tamping down his urge to gather her into his arms.

Karen had never been smitten by men with stubbled beards, but on Zed the stubble added a dangerous aura that fascinated her. Especially when he gazed at her so hungrily. Involuntarily she took a step toward him.

"We seem to keep sharing beds," he said softly. "I'm not sure I can keep doing that and behaving." He held out his hands and she put her hands into his, allowing him to draw her closer, until they were almost but not quite touching.

"What I'm saying is," he continued, "we'll probably be staying in Monterey for a few days while Danny recuperates. This place is convenient to the hospital."

"It's fine," she said, trying to control her breathing and concentrate on what he was saying. When he was this close to her, she had trouble thinking.

"Then you want to stay here until we can take Danny home?"

She nodded, her gaze fixed on his lips. How was it she'd never noticed the elegant curve of his upper lip and the sensual fullness of the lower?

"We do have a problem, then."

"No problem," she murmured, wondering when he was going to kiss her.

"If you say it's not, I sure as hell won't argue." He set down the mug he carried and lowered his head until his lips met hers.

His stubble rasped against her face, not unpleasantly, adding a new dimension to his kiss. Her lips parted, allowing him entry, and she tasted coffee as well as his own special flavor. He gathered her to him, his hands sliding down to cup her rear, pressing her against his arousal while he nibbled at her lips, his tongue tasting and exploring her mouth.

Desire raced like wildfire along her nerves, diffusing through her, flushing her skin and turning her insides molten. She wrapped her arms around him, responding to his kiss with a passion she'd never felt before for any man.

They swayed together, so intense was the desire bonding them. She felt that if he released her she'd melt into a pool at his feet. She slid her hands under his shirt, eager to touch his skin.

He groaned, lifting her off her feet and carrying her the few steps to the ornate brass bed. Just as they sprawled together on it, she heard the tinkle of a bell. Faint at first, the ringing grew louder and more insistent, making it impossible to ignore.

Zed pulled away from her enough to mutter, "I take it that means breakfast is served. To hell with breakfast. You're what I need."

She needed him, too, but if they didn't appear, Karen feared the next summons might be a knock at their door. Sighing, she eased free and stood, saying, "From the tone of that bell, I'd say the ringer means it as a warning—you'd better eat or else. Now.''

Before they went downstairs Karen made a valiant attempt to do what she could to appear fresh and neat despite the lack of a brush and having to wear the same clothes she'd slept in.

The breakfast, served in three courses, was so delicious it was almost but not quite worth forgoing what the bell had interrupted—but then, she hadn't had anything to eat since the previous noon. She was so hungry she didn't even try to make polite conversation with the other six guests at the table.

The owner, whose name was Mrs. Haven, beamed at Karen and Zed as they left the table. ''The best praise of a cook is an empty plate,'' she said when Karen complimented her on the food.

''We'll be staying another night,'' Zed said. ''Possibly two or more, depending on when the doctors decide to release Danny.''

At his words, the penny dropped and Karen realized exactly what she'd tacitly agreed to in her bemused state upstairs. They'd be in the same room, sharing the same bed, and Zed couldn't be expected to sleep on top of the covers again. A thrill shot through her at the image that evoked.

Mrs. Haven's smile faded. ''I do hope your son improves rapidly. You seem to be such a nice young couple.''

Deciding there was no point in trying to straighten things out, Karen merely thanked her for her concern. After all, they might not be husband and wife, as Mrs. Haven assumed, but they *were* a couple, temporary though it might be. And Danny might not be Zed's son but in every way that counted, he was hers.

At the hospital she couldn't wait to get to Danny's room, berating herself for stopping to eat. She should have rushed right over here the moment she awoke. He needed her—if he was awake he'd be miserable at finding himself among strangers. The poor sweetie didn't even have his beloved blue horse to console him.

She rushed into his room ahead of Zed and stopped short, staring at the scene in front of her. A nurse sat in a rocker beside the crib holding Danny on her lap while he contentedly sucked on a bottle. Though the bruise over his left forehead and temple had spread so that he had a black eye, he didn't seem to be in pain. Zed, meanwhile, walked past her, halting beside the rocker and crouching down to Danny's level.

"Hi, Tiger," he said. "You look like a prizefighter who got the worst of it."

Danny focused on him, pushing the nipple from his mouth and trying to reach toward him. The nurse handed the boy to Zed, who settled him into the crook of his arm. "Look," he said, turning Danny toward where she still stood, "there's Mama."

"Ma," Danny said, holding out his arms to her.

Tears filled Karen's eyes as she took him from Zed, holding Danny to her, trying not to hug him too tightly. "Thank God," she whispered, too full of emotion to speak.

Later, as she walked around carrying Danny, she watched him smile at the nurse who'd been holding him. "Ga," he said to the nurse. "Ga, ga."

"My name's Georgia," she told Karen. "I said my

name to him four or five times while I was bathing and feeding him this morning and, after we got to know each other, he began babbling, saying 'Ga ga.' I know at seven months he's probably too young to direct his verbal skills, but I like to think he's trying to say my name. He's a real doll.''

Karen talked to Georgia for a few minutes, belatedly noticing that Zed had slipped from the room. No doubt for more coffee—he was a real caffeine fiend.

''How do you convince a man who's into caffeine to ease up?'' she asked the nurse.

''Nothing worked for me at first,'' Georgia told her. ''My husband ignored all the statistics and so on. So what I finally resorted to was to dilute his coffee with decaf while it was still unbrewed in the can—stir it well and you can't see any difference. I used just a little decaf at first and, when he didn't seem to notice, gradually increased it. I'm up to half and half now. I know it's sneaky, but if he won't watch his health, I darn well will.''

Clever but, even if she had the chance, Karen doubted that Zed would appreciate being hoodwinked. And, of course, she would never have the chance if she did decide to try Georgia's method.

Zed, drawn to ICU as though by invisible threads, took a deep breath before entering the 5A cubicle. He stepped to the bed. Talal looked much as he had early this morning, lying still with closed eyes, hooked up to various devices, his left leg in a cast.

''Talal?'' Zed said softly.

The injured man's eyes opened and he blinked.

"Zeid!" he exclaimed. "Was it your blood they gave me?"

Staggered anew by hearing Talal say his name, Zed managed a feeble "Yes."

"No matter what they told me as a child," Talal said, "I knew Zeid was real. I knew you were real." He shifted position, grimacing as though moving was painful. "How did you find me?"

"What do you mean, I was real?" Zed demanded, shocked from his bemusement.

Talal was silent for a long moment. "You didn't remember at all, did you?" He spoke sadly.

The vision of sand and a ball flashed before Zed and, without thinking, he blurted, "A red ball. I remember that much and no more. The ball and sand."

"What you recall is Kholi. Our country is sand. And the ball was yours. Mine was yellow. I still have them both."

Zed leaned against the side rail of Talal's bed. "I don't understand."

"My friend, my brother, I am too tired to explain. You must tell me how, knowing nothing of me, you came to donate your blood to save my life."

"I donated the blood for Danny." Zed paused abruptly. Whoever else Talal was, he was Danny's father. How was he to explain the situation to a man not yet fully recovered from the surgery that had repaired his serious injuries?

"Danny?" Talal echoed. Louie in San Diego had been right, Zed thought. Talal spoke excellent English, with only a slight accent.

Wondering how to word his explanation, he remembered advice of his grandmother's. When Jade rattled on as a child, Grandma would say, "Begin at the beginning so I can understand what you're talking about. The beginning is always the best place to start." He'd start there.

"You remember Erin Henderson?" he asked.

Talal frowned. "Erin? Erin?"

Zed didn't believe he was faking. Either he really couldn't place her or the boat accident had disturbed his memory. "She had red hair."

Talal's face cleared. "Now I recall her. In San Diego we sailed together for a time."

Listening to his offhand words, Zed found himself convinced Talal hadn't known about Erin's pregnancy. Gazing down at his sunken eyes with the dark circles around them, Zed shook his head. The man was obviously very weak, in no condition to face what he had to tell him. "Look," he said, "you're not in the greatest shape. I'll come back when you've had a chance to recuperate from the surgery."

"No!" The word snapped like a whip from Talal's lips. "I'm not too ill to listen. I must know. You will tell me now."

Feeling a strange sense of déjà vu, as though Talal had commanded him before, Zed, against his better judgment, went on, condensing his explanation. "Apparently you and Erin were careless. She became pregnant. Danny is her son. Your son."

For a moment the sunken eyes flashed fire. "I have no sons!"

As calmly as he could, Zed said, "Danny's blood is an exact match with yours. You both carry some oddball component that the docs tell me is very rare."

"As you do."

Zed nodded. Thinking he knew what was fomenting in Talal's mind, he said, "I never met Erin Henderson and I never will, because she died bearing Danny. Her cousin, Karen, tracked me down on the basis of a photo of you and Erin aboard the *Maddamti*. Because we look alike, the private detective Karen hired mistook me for you. Since then, Karen and I have been searching for you by trying to trace the *Maddamti*."

Talal closed his eyes, remaining silent. Exhausted or shutting him out? Zed wondered.

"Danny?" Talal asked without opening his eyes. "The blood you donated?"

"Karen and I were in an accident driving to Monterey in the storm that put you and the *Maddamti* on the rocks. We weren't hurt, but Danny was. I donated blood in case he had to have surgery. Luckily he didn't. You did, so they were able to use the blood for you."

"We match, you and I and Danny. He looks like us?"

"He resembles my sister, Jade, more than me."

Talal's eyes flew open and his hand shot out to grip the handrail. "A sister named Jaida?"

"Jade."

"I don't want to lose you, but I must rest before I can process a son and a sister," Talal said. "You will return."

Though it was more an order than a question, Zed nodded. "I'll be back. You still owe me an explanation."

He left ICU, his mind whirling with questions. Talal had called him his friend and his brother. Merely an Arab phrase or the truth? Zed shook his head. He was no Arab. He'd never been in Kholi—or any other Middle Eastern country, for that matter.

How could Talal Zohir possibly be his brother?

Chapter Ten

At the hospital, Karen, concentrating on Danny, vaguely noted that Zed seemed distracted but, since he'd gotten up far earlier than she had, she put it down to lack of sleep and forgot about it.

Sometime during the morning he disappeared to check on the wrecked car. When he returned to the hospital he carried Danny's bedraggled blue horse. She expected the boy to drop the octopus and hug his beloved favorite to him, but to her surprise he transferred the octopus to his right hand and grasped the horse with his left.

"Atta boy," Zed told him. "When offered a choice, you can't go wrong by taking both."

Danny promptly dropped both the stuffed toys and picked up a bright red plastic cylinder that rattled and chimed when he shook it.

"Georgia gave it to him," Karen said. "She's his

nurse. I think they've begun a mutual admiration society."

"A guy can't begin too young," Zed observed.

"What about my car?" she asked. "I suppose it was totaled."

Zed nodded. "Your insurance company won't argue about that. I rented a car for us to get around in and brought our belongings to Snug Haven."

Dr. Nelson stepped into the room, nodding to them as he crossed to Danny's crib. The boy stopped playing with the chiming toy and gazed solemnly up at the doctor.

"Hello, snicklefritz," Dr. Nelson said as he let down the crib rail. "That's some shiner you've got there." With slow and gentle movements he proceeded to peer into Danny's eyes. Other than casting anxious looks at Karen, the boy submitted without either fighting or crying.

"What about his black eye?" Karen asked.

"Like the blood clot inside the skull, the external bruising will resorb," the doctor assured her. "I can't guarantee it, but I doubt he'll have any permanent damage. We tested him early this morning and the clot is definitely shrinking. If all goes well he may be ready to leave the hospital by tomorrow."

"That's good news," Zed said.

Dr. Nelson finished his examination of Danny and put up the crib side. "I'll send a summary of Danny's injuries along with you to give to his doctor in San Diego," he continued. "Danny will need a few follow-up visits there."

"I'll see to that," Karen declared. "His recovery seems like a miracle. I'm so grateful to you."

"All I did was stand by and allow nature to begin the healing," Dr. Nelson said. "Danny's doing the rest."

Karen smiled at the doctor's modesty. Nature might be healing Danny, but Dr. Nelson's years of training had given him the expertise to know when his intervention wasn't necessary.

"Which reminds me," the doctor added, turning his attention to Zed.

At that moment Danny began fussing, so Karen lifted him into her arms. Attempting to soothe him, she missed part of what Dr. Nelson was saying to Zed.

"...your blood made the difference," the doctor finished. "The orthopedic surgeon tells me he's doing very well." He nodded to Karen. "I'll see you tomorrow morning."

"What was that all about?" she asked after the doctor left the room.

"Da," Danny said, reaching toward Zed.

She relinquished her hold, watching with pleasure as Danny eased into Zed's arms and reached up to pat his cheek. It still amazed her how patient he was with the baby.

"Since Danny didn't need the blood I donated," he said, "they asked my permission to give it to an injured man heading for emergency surgery. I agreed."

Karen started to compliment him on being generous. Then the words died on her lips as a thought struck her. "But you've got special blood, haven't you? You and Danny."

He nodded. "That's why they needed my blood. The man was—is—Danny's father. Talal Zohir. Apparently our blood matches his. I kept meaning to tell you but, well, the time just never came."

She stared at him, astounded at the news and a bit hurt that he hadn't told her earlier. "Are you saying Talal Zohir is a patient in this hospital?"

"During the storm the *Maddamti* piled up on some rocks at the bay entrance. Dr. Nelson said Talal shattered his ankle, broke a leg bone and lost quite a bit of blood in the accident."

About to ask him if he'd seen or talked to Talal, she held. Obviously he hadn't. How could he, if Talal had been so badly injured as to need emergency surgery? Shaking her head, she said, "I'm having trouble grasping that Talal Zohir is actually within reach. I wonder if he'll be recovered enough by tomorrow for us to visit him."

"I imagine he will." Zed's tone sounded grim, making her curious why.

"Now that we've found him, he has to be told about Danny," she declared. "He has to face up to his responsibilities." She scowled. "I need to know why he deserted Erin."

"Maybe he didn't. It's entirely possible Talal never knew about the pregnancy."

Karen blinked. "You sound as though you're on his side."

"You told me yourself that Erin was irresponsible. She may never have contacted him."

Much as she hated to admit it, Zed did have a point, one she didn't like to acknowledge because it seemed traitorous. Poor Erin was dead because of Talal Zohir—how could Zed possibly imagine she'd give him the benefit of the doubt?

"I certainly expect him to act responsibly now," she said, conceding nothing.

Zed remained silent. Disturbed at his lack of response, she prodded him. "Don't you agree?"

He walked to the window with Danny and stood there staring out. "Wait," he said without turning to face her.

Wait? Did he mean for his answer? Or was he advising her to wait until she confronted Talal? She took a deep breath and let it out slowly. Zed had a point. After all, Talal was an injured man, lucky to have survived his accident. She had to remember to take that into consideration when they met.

She was about to join Zed at the window when a sound at the door made her pause. She looked around and saw a male attendant pushing a man in a wheelchair into the room, a bearded man with his leg extended in a cast. The attendant left him there and exited. She drew in her breath, rocked back on her heels at what she saw before her. A photo was one thing, the man in the flesh another. Involuntarily she glanced toward Zed, who was turning from the window. If that man had a beard—!

"Twins?" she blurted.

"The lady is more perceptive than you, Zeid," Talal observed.

Zed, carrying Danny, walked toward Talal. Ignoring both her exclamation and Talal's remark, he said, "This is your son. Erin's child."

Danny gazed suspiciously at Talal, then held out his arms to Karen. Zed handed him over. Clinging to her, Danny regarded Talal uneasily.

"Is the boy all right?" Talal asked her.

Speechless, she nodded.

"We can't be twins," Zed told Talal. "It's impossible."

"I can't offer you proof, but in my heart I know the truth. We are one, split in two by Allah's will." Talal spoke with such complete finality that Karen found herself on the verge of believing him.

"I've never been in Kholi," Zed said. "I was born in California. My birth certificate says so."

"I don't yet know how it is possible, but I will find out. Is not your name Zeid?"

"Zed."

Talal shrugged. "An Americanization of Zeid." He shifted his gaze to Karen. "You are Erin's cousin?"

Again she nodded, not trusting herself to speak.

"Erin and I lost touch," Talal said. "She didn't inform me she was pregnant." He reached up from the wheelchair as though to touch Danny but didn't complete the motion, letting his hand fall back onto the arm of the chair. "The blood match suggests he could be my son. We shall see."

Something about his manner put Karen off. Imperious was the word that came to her. A man who expected others to obey him. "Danny *is* your son," she insisted, determined not to let him cow her.

"Perhaps. It will be investigated." He switched his attention back to Zed. "My brother, I can't explain how it is that you were born in California and I in Kholi but I intend to get to the bottom of this matter." He turned toward the partly open door. "Nurse!" he called. "I'm ready to go."

The young man appeared in the doorway and, without

a word of farewell, Talal allowed himself to be wheeled away.

Karen looked at Zed, expecting him to share her bemusement, and found him scowling. "That damn red ball," he muttered, confusing her.

"You and Talal do look enough alike to be twins," she said. "Could he be the half brother you suspected might exist?"

"I've considered that. I just don't know."

"You'll have to question him. Ask him what his father's name was and whether he was an Arab. He didn't have to be. Oil brought a lot of American men to the Middle East a few years back."

Zed shook his head. "Since I don't know my father's name, that might not help. But I intend to get to the bottom of this."

For a moment he sounded so much like Talal she was startled by the similarity. There might be no proof, but she felt in her bones that the two men were related. The nurse came in with Danny's lunch, distracting her. Only later, after he was fed and napping, did it occur to her that the meeting between Zed and Talal hadn't been quite right, though she wasn't able to put her finger on the reason.

Zed offered to stay with Danny while she returned to Snug Haven to change into clean clothes, and as she walked the two blocks she mulled it over. What had been wrong in that meeting?

Though she couldn't cite a single incident that led to her conviction, she grew more and more positive that this hadn't been their first contact. If this was true, why had Zed concealed it from her? Was his offer to remain at the hospital made because he meant to talk to Talal again without her present? Could it have anything to do with Danny?

Unease hastened her steps. She reached their room, showered and changed clothes, slipping into a denim skirt and knit shirt before heading back to the hospital. She half expected to find Zed wasn't in Danny's room, but she found him slumped in the rocker asleep. Looking down at him, helpless and unaware for the moment, she felt her heart ache with tenderness. How could she have doubted him?

Yet a tendril of suspicion remained coiled in her mind.

After leaving the hospital in the evening, they drove to a seafood café recommended by one of the nurses and, once they finished eating, returned to Snug Haven.

Since she'd agreed up front to share the room with Zed, Karen hadn't expected her sudden attack of shyness and uncertainty. As she changed into her admittedly sheer and frivolous short nightgown in the bathroom, she tentatively reached for her terry robe, then shook her head. If she wore it he'd know she was having second thoughts. Or sort of, anyway. When she hesitantly emerged, his frankly admiring gaze lifted her heart but at the same time increased her shyness.

She watched him disappear into the bathroom, then glanced around the room, seeking she wasn't sure what. The unopened jar of peanut butter caught her eye. She loved the stuff, but decided she was too tense to swallow even water, much less sticky peanut butter.

Climbing into bed might be misconstrued as seeming too eager. Was she? Yes and no. On tenterhooks, she finally retreated to the window and looked out at the star-studded night sky. The moon hadn't risen, always supposing the moon meant to show itself tonight. She'd lost track of its waxing and waning.

That wasn't all she'd lost track of. Her entire life had been totally disrupted since she'd met Zed. She'd never be the same. She had so many things to worry about—Danny's future, Talal's reception of her accusation—yet, at the moment, everything except Zed lacked importance. He occupied her mind to the exclusion of all else.

"An inspiring sight." Zed spoke from behind her and she started.

"I didn't hear you," she accused, turning.

"I like to creep up on pretty ladies," he said, grinning. "Especially scantily clad ones named Karen."

Surreptitiously she examined him. Gone were the old gray sweats. Instead he wore what looked to be a new pair of deep red pajamas—just the pants—of course hanging dangerously low on his hips rather than fitting snugly at his waist. She wished she was brave enough to tell him how beautiful his body was, but the words wouldn't come.

"Zed," she confessed, "I'm scared."

His eyebrows rose. "Scared? Of me?"

"Well, maybe nervous is a better word."

He took her hands in his and raised them to his lips, sending a delightful frisson running along her spine. Then he released her hands and offered her one of his. She clasped his hand in both of hers and, without pausing to think about what she meant to do, caressed his fingers one by one, marveling at the calluses on his palm, a working man's hand. Though she didn't understand why, touching his hand so intimately seemed to connect her to him in a way she'd never felt with any other man.

He led her to the big brass bed, then lifted her onto it. Seating himself at her feet, he ran his fingers over her toes, then began massaging her soles and insteps. As he did so, she felt herself relaxing under his expert touch. After a time she said, "Now, you."

As she massaged his feet, she did her best to offer him the pleasure he'd given her and felt rewarded when he sighed.

Next he had her lie on her stomach and, easing his hands under her short gown, gave her a back rub, using long, lazy strokes from her nape down over her buttocks and thighs, his massage both relaxing and erotic. Though he confined himself to her back, she felt his stroking all over her body.

By the time she straddled him to rub his back, she'd lost all self-consciousness, aware only of the wonderful feel of his skin under her hands, warm and soft over the hard muscles just beneath.

When he turned over unexpectedly, toppling her onto her side, she was more than ready—she was eager to be enfolded in his arms. Pulling her close, he kissed her lightly, tender kisses that nibbled delicately at her lips, adding fuel to the slow inner heat his back rub had ignited.

"Mmm," she murmured, snuggling closer as she used the tip of her tongue to taste him, running it along his lips until they parted and then venturing inside. She could taste faint traces of the mint the restaurant had served with the bill, but underneath she savored his special flavor, belonging to him alone.

He deepened the kiss, entangling her tongue with his

until she was breathless with desire and burning with wanting. His hand cupped her breast, his thumb caressing her turgid nipple through the thin material of her gown. She gasped with pleasure when he slid his hand underneath the gown and touched her bare breast.

In a flurry of need, pajama pants, gown and bikini panties were flung aside and they lay skin-to-skin, flesh-to-flesh. His crinkly chest hair teased her nipples until he crushed her to him, his arousal hot and throbbing against her thigh, turning her insides to liquid.

His hands slid over her, his touch arousing her until she moaned with the sweet intensity of her desire. "Zed," she entreated. "Please, Zed."

"Tell me what you want," he murmured.

She wanted more, she wanted everything. "You," she gasped.

His fingers found her molten center, sending indescribable thrills through her. Moments later he rose above her, easing between her legs. She opened to him and when he entered her she cried out, feeling a passion so fierce she was unable to contain herself. Gripping him close, she unconsciously matched the rhythm of his thrusts as they traveled higher and higher together until they reached the summit.

Afterward he held her, gently brushing back strands of hair that had fallen across her face. "Karen," he murmured, "My beautiful Karen."

His Karen. He'd said those words once before, and then, as now, they made her heart sing. For this space of time, at least, she *was* his in the same way that he was hers. No man had ever evoked such passion in her. Perhaps because she felt more than physical desire for him.

The word *love* trembled on the edge of her thoughts, sending a shock wave through her.

This was no time to fall in love! He'd made no promises, no commitments, and she'd always vowed never to allow herself to love a man until she could be sure they had some kind of a future together. Apparently, though, love couldn't be contained by rules—hers or anyone else's.

He traced her lips with his forefinger. "Still scared?"

If she told the truth, yes. But now she really had something to be afraid of. Not him, never him. Zed was the most wonderful lover she could imagine. Her own feelings were what frightened her.

Had her cousin felt this way about Talal Zohir? Though it was difficult for her to picture butterfly Erin alighting in any one involvement long enough to be caught in the web of love, wasn't it possible? Just because she hadn't cared for Talal's manner didn't mean Erin would have had the same reaction toward him.

"Too scared to speak?" Zed asked.

In answer, she rose on her elbow, leaned over and brushed his lips with what she intended as a light, ephemeral kiss, a kiss not meant to be in any way arousing. But the softness of his lips under hers made her linger long enough for him to respond, and she discovered the inner coals of desire were still burning, ready to burst into flame.

As their kiss deepened, Zed shifted Karen until she lay on top of him; he relished the erotic sensation of her nakedness against his. How smooth and soft her skin was, how tempting the curves of her beautiful body, how arousing her kisses.

Once with her had been far from enough. The way she made him feel, he doubted twice would suffice, either. How many times would be enough? Setting that problem aside for the moment—with her in his arms, who wanted to think?—he eased her onto her side so he could indulge his need to tease her nipple with his tongue. Her taste was addictive. So was her scent—flowery and feminine and only hers.

She'd driven him wild earlier when her shy responses turned to heated passion. It had been all he could do to hold back until she was ready. There was nothing shy about her caresses now, and she was still making him crazy with need. No woman had ever made him feel such intense desire. He never wanted to let her go; he wanted to plunge inside her and stay there forever, rocking on the verge of completion.

Her tiny moans and the way she moved against him told him she was as eager as he. When she breathed, "Please" in his ear, he didn't hesitate. His passion completely out of control, he took her and himself to a peak he'd never before scaled.

Even afterward he was reluctant to release her. All the old cliché phrases he'd ever heard were true, damn it. She'd gotten under his skin, into his blood; she held him in thrall with that old black magic; he'd begin the beguine with her any old time.

She reached to caress his cheek and his heart melted. What the hell was happening to him? He was uneasily aware that a four-letter word existed for the way she made him feel, but he couldn't believe it was happening to him. Love? Get real!

They fell asleep, still entwined. He roused to daylight

and reached for her, only to find she wasn't in the bed. In the bathroom the shower was running. Triggered by visions of jumping into the shower with her, he leapt up and tried the door, but found it locked. Another time, he told himself consolingly. Another time—soon.

As he waited for her to finish, the problem of Talal slid into his mind. Preoccupied with making love to and with Karen, Zed had successfully shut him out until now. But his relationship to Talal was a problem that wouldn't go away, a problem he had to solve.

Were they brothers? The blood match suggested they must be. Or maybe half brothers, linked by a father. Certainly not twins, as Talal insisted. How could that be when they'd been born in different countries? Impossible!

What about the tenuous link he'd been aware of from the moment he stared down at the unconscious Talal? Why had Talal said he knew Zed was real, knew he existed, no matter what they'd told him. Who were "they"?

With these questions circling in his mind, he couldn't wait to get to the hospital so Talal could provide him with some answers. When Karen was finished he showered and dressed rapidly, finishing in an even tie with her. "Why do women take so long to get ready?" he teased.

"Because men judge us by how we look instead of by what we are," she answered.

He grinned at her. "So far you check out in all areas. You even appeal to me grungy."

She made a face at him, and it was all he could do not to wrap his arms around her and kiss her breathless. But that would lead to something else and they'd never get under way. He had to get to the hospital.

Mrs. Haven's breakfast was as delicious as the day before. When they were finished, Zed told her he wasn't sure about the room, because Danny might be discharged.

"Don't let it worry you," she told him. "You can let me know when you know."

At the hospital Zed went with Karen to check out Danny and found Georgia, the nurse, playing peekaboo with him. Reassured that the boy was all right, he told Karen, "I'm going to talk to Talal."

At ICU he learned Talal had been transferred to the men's surgical ward. When he reached that floor, he was told Talal was no longer a patient at the hospital.

"You mean the doctor discharged him already?" Zed asked, aghast.

"I believe Mr. Zohir signed himself out against the doctor's advice," the ward clerk replied. "In any case, he's not here."

Further questioning turned up Bob, the male attendant who'd helped Talal get ready to leave. "I wheeled him down to the limo he'd booked," Bob said. "I understood that the limo was taking him to the airport because he'd chartered a plane for New York. Dr. Longworth, the surgeon who operated on him, was mad as hell, but there was no stopping him." He took another look at Zed. "You his brother?" Bob asked.

Zed settled for a nod, since it was more believable than admitting he didn't know.

Bob spread his hands. "All I can say is he didn't leave any message for you. Or for anyone else."

Disturbed and confused, Zed took his time returning to pediatrics. When he entered Danny's room, Karen was sitting in the rocker holding the boy. "Da!" Danny cried.

"Hello to you, too, Tiger," Zed said, forcing a smile for Danny.

"Well?" Karen asked. "What did Talal have to say?"

"He's gone." His words dropped like stones into a mine shaft.

Karen blinked. "What do you mean, gone? Did something happen to him?"

Zed shook his head. "Nothing catastrophic. He signed himself out of the hospital, hired a limo to drive him to the airport, and took a plane to New York."

She stared at him. "He must have left you a message."

"Nope, nothing."

For a moment Karen looked as confused as he felt, then her expression darkened. "He ran out, didn't he? Ran out on you and his responsibility to Danny. I didn't like him or trust him from the moment I set eyes on him, and I was right. I've been right all along. He's a weasling no-good."

"Don't say that!" Zed's annoyed response surprised him, as well as obviously taking Karen aback.

She bristled. "It's the truth. Talal can't be trusted. I'll lay odds he's not staying in New York but will be flying on home to Kholi to get well beyond our reach. He's deliberately turned his back on both you and Danny."

Zed tried to tamp down his irritation at Karen, telling himself she didn't understand. "Talal wouldn't do that," he said as calmly as he could. "He's not that kind of man."

"How can you say that?" she cried. "You just met him. He may be some sort of relative of yours, but you don't have a clue about what kind of person he is. Well,

I do! He already deserted my cousin. What makes you so sure he wouldn't do the same thing to you and Danny?''

"I can't explain.'' Zed found it impossible to keep his growing anger from creeping into his voice. "Irrational though it may seem to you, I feel in my bones that he wouldn't behave dishonorably. It isn't in him to run away.''

Karen made a small disgusted sound. "Even though that's exactly what he did.''

Zed clamped his lips shut. There was no point in trying to convince Karen that he was certain Talal would be back. How he knew this was beyond him, but he'd never felt more sure of anything in his life. In some way he didn't yet comprehend, he and Talal were linked.

Chapter Eleven

In spite of Zed's reluctance to argue, the dispute between Karen and Zed in Danny's hospital room continued until the boy started to cry, upset by their raised voices. As Karen tried to soothe him, Georgia came in with a message from Dr. Nelson.

"The doctor's tied up in surgery," she said. "He won't be able to get here to see Danny until late afternoon. He doesn't want to let him go without examining him, so he asks that you please be patient."

Karen and Zed looked at each other in dismay. It wasn't so much that she was upset about the doctor, Karen thought. She didn't mind waiting. What bothered her was having to hang around all day with Zed when she was so irked with him that she had the urge to slam his head against the wall in an attempt to knock some sense into it.

From the look on his face, he felt the same way about her.

Georgia went out. As Danny quieted down, Karen decided that, rather than get into another argument, she would keep her mouth shut. A silence fell, broken only by Danny's babbling.

"Care for something to eat?" Zed asked finally.

She shook her head, not caring at the moment if she ever ate again.

"Decaf?" he persisted.

"No, thank you," she said coolly. "Nothing."

She expected him to go out to get himself coffee and maybe a snack but, instead, he crossed to the window and stared out. "The side of another building isn't the most inspiring view," he remarked after a time.

Since no reply was required, she said nothing.

At last he turned to face her. "I think I'll call Jade and update her," he said.

"That's a good idea," she said politely. His sister certainly deserved to be caught up on what had happened, and the call would get him out of her hair for a while. She watched him leave the room.

She couldn't understand why he defended Talal so vehemently. Why wasn't he able to see what was so obvious to her? The man had fled to Kholi to avoid the situation. Once in Kholi, he could never be brought to account, never be forced to acknowledge his son in any way.

Sitting down in the rocker, she settled Danny onto her lap and said, "You didn't like Talal either, did you?"

Danny gazed at her, offering her one of his sweet smiles. His bruises had begun to fade to ghastly greens and yellows, marking improvement, she knew, but it made the poor little guy look terrible. She hugged him, saying, "We don't need that mean old Talal, anyway. We'll get along just fine."

"Da?" he said.

"No, that's Zed," she told him without thinking, only realizing after the words were out that it was true. In every way that mattered, Zed behaved like Danny's father. Too bad he wasn't.

When Zed returned to the room, having decided to try to act reasonably despite their marked difference of opinion, she asked, "How is your sister?"

"Swamped."

When he didn't elaborate, she decided he was still annoyed with her. Well, even if he couldn't rise above his irritation and be reasonable, she could keep her cool and remain polite.

"Did Jade land the big contract?" she asked.

"Yes."

With effort Karen refrained from scowling at him. She was determined not to react to his terseness. At the same time she was damned if she meant to let him get away with it. No way!

Keeping her tone calm and even, she said, "Then that must be what you were referring to when you said she was swamped—right?"

For the first time since coming back, he looked directly at her. "Partly. There are a few other problems."

His dark eyes that only last night had been so tender and loving were now as hard and cold as obsidian. In order to conceal her upset at being treated like an enemy, she shifted her gaze to Danny. Refusing to be cowed, she said, "I imagine Jade was surprised to know we'd found

Danny's father." She bit her tongue to stop herself from adding, *and lost him.*

"She was relieved."

Karen shot him a speculative look. *I'll bet you didn't even tell her Talal skipped the country,* she thought, but didn't say so.

"I hope Dr. Nelson discharges Danny today," Zed said.

She did, too. Surely he knew that.

"Da," Danny crowed, holding his arms up toward Zed. For a long moment she didn't think Zed meant to respond, then he shook his head, as though throwing off his dark mood, and smiled at the boy.

"Hey, Tiger, time for our man-to-man thing—right?" As he spoke he lifted the boy from her lap, carrying him to the window. "Not much to see but, look, there's a bird, a pigeon, landing on the windowsill. Pigeons like bread crumbs, so if we had some bread and opened the window we could feed it."

A moment later he added, "I guess the bird knows we don't have a handout—look, it's flying away. That's what birds do, you know, fly." His tone, talking to the boy, was warm and affectionate.

She bit back the tart observation that birds weren't the only things that flew—Talal had taken flight, as well.

As the morning dragged on, she and Zed remained in an armed truce, not resuming their argument—because, she was positive, of her forbearance. Eventually, Danny had his lunch and fell asleep.

"We haven't eaten," Zed said then. "He's napping. No need for either of us to be here."

"I'm not particularly hungry," she responded. "And I don't want to miss Dr. Nelson. Maybe the cafeteria—"

Zed glanced at his watch. "It's only twelve-thirty. Georgia said the doctor wouldn't be here until late afternoon, so we have a couple of hours to kill. Believe me, the hospital cafeteria is to be avoided. If you don't want to go far and don't care for a lot to eat, remember we have crackers and peanut butter in our room. I bought cheese and soft drinks, too."

She took his words as a peace offering of sorts. Besides, though she wanted to be with Danny when he was awake, being stuck in his room while he napped wasn't appealing. And peanut butter *was* a favorite of hers. She'd almost opened the jar last night. "Sounds good," she admitted.

When they left the hospital she was surprised to find the day shrouded in mist. "The sun was out when we walked over this morning," she protested.

"This tends to be a foggy coastline," he said. "Beautiful as it is, the Monterey peninsula isn't high on my list of good sailing spots."

"What places do you like the best?" she asked, glad they'd found a neutral subject.

He was describing Emerald Bay on Lake Tahoe in glowing terms when they reached Snug Haven. "Positively awesome in midsummer on a moonlit night," he finished. "I'll show you someday."

Her heart leapt at the thought of spending a night anchored in a beautiful bay with the moon shining down on them. On her and Zed. With an effort she banished the image from her mind. It wasn't likely to happen. His words meant no more than a casual acquaintance saying, "We must get together for lunch sometime."

Except Zed wasn't merely a casual acquaintance. At least, as far as she was concerned.

Mrs. Haven looked into the hall when they entered, and Zed spoke to her. "It looks like we'll be staying here another night, but we may need a crib in the room."

With her assurance the crib would be put in place whether or not they came back with Danny, they mounted the stairs. Thinking about the crib, Karen told herself she was relieved Danny would probably be playing chaperon. With this unresolved Talal argument still smoldering between them, she certainly didn't want to make love with Zed tonight.

In the room she discovered that Zed had hit on her favorite brand of saltines as well as peanut butter, plus he'd remembered to buy plastic knives to use for spreading. She smiled at him in approval as she spread a cracker with a generous serving of peanut butter while he opened an orange soft drink for her.

"This feels like an indoor picnic," she said, sitting on the floor with her goodies and leaning up against the bed.

"Exactly my thought. A picnic lunch." As he picked up the cheese and peeled off its wrapping, she noticed the box of arrowroot biscuits and her heart melted. He'd even thought of Danny.

He sat on the floor with his stack of cheese and crackers and his cola drink.

"Caffeine all the way," she remarked.

He slanted her an unrepentant grin. "Warms the cockles of a man's heart."

"I thought that was whiskey."

"I never said there wasn't more than one drink capable of the warming." His gaze softened and she felt herself being drawn into the deep, soft darkness of his eyes. "Nor did I point out there was something far more potent than caffeine or whiskey, something capable of not only warming a man's heart but his soul, as well.''

With some difficulty she shook off her bemusement and took another bite of her cracker, telling herself she was not going to be seduced by his eyes.

"If you give me a taste of yours, you can have a taste of mine," he said.

She shot him a look of mock reproof. "My mother taught me never to eat off anyone else's plate."

"Who's got plates?" he asked, offering her a bite of his cheese and cracker without releasing it.

She leaned forward and took a bite, crumbs scattering onto the floor. "Mrs. Haven will be annoyed," she said after she swallowed it.

"What're a few crumbs? Overall, we're rather neat," he countered. "Now it's my turn." Grasping her hand, the one holding the remnants of her cracker, he took the rest of the cracker from her hand with his mouth, the warmth of his lips teasing her fingers.

He swallowed the bite and leaned toward her. "That's not all I need to taste," he said softly as his lips met hers.

Never mind that they'd argued, never mind that she'd told herself she wasn't going to succumb to any attempt at lovemaking. The reality of his mouth on hers banished everything else. He was what she needed to taste, to kiss, to hold. To love. Now.

Zed seethed with his need for her. He fought for enough control to keep from easing her to the floor and taking her without any preliminaries. Karen deserved the best he could give. Stubborn she might be, as well as irritatingly unreasonable—but that didn't matter. Whatever Karen was, he wanted her to be his. Now.

She felt so soft against him, soft and warm and utterly desirable. He hadn't consciously suggested this indoor picnic with making love in mind, but he couldn't deny the idea might have been hidden somewhere in his mind. He also couldn't deny it was a great idea.

Her skin was so much fairer than his, so white and delicate. Her eyes were the color the ocean sometimes took on, neither a true blue nor an absolute green—a beautiful shade. If he wasn't driven by such intense need, he could gaze into those eyes for hours. Her body fit against him as though it was made for that purpose and her breasts were perfectly shaped to fit his hands. With Karen in his arms, the world faded away. She became the only thing that mattered.

After a time, caressing her through layers of cloth grew frustrating. Pushing aside the obstacle of her clothes, he put his mouth to her breast, taking in the pale pink nipple that hardened as his tongue flicked over it. Her soft moans of pleasure ignited him, driving him to more intimate caresses.

With delirious pleasure he felt her hands undressing him; he was thrilled by the knowledge she wanted him as much as he wanted her, that she was driven by the same urgent need. All her emotions were genuine—passion, anger, affection. There was nothing fake about her. She was a woman to be trusted.

She was a woman to be loved. Or did he mean a woman to make love with? Which is what he was doing and would like to do forever if it were humanly possible. The more he held her, the more he wanted her.

When at last they lay flesh-to-flesh, the exquisite feel of her naked body drove him up and up until he reached the point of no return. Answering her whispered plea of "Please," he rose over her. Settling himself between her thighs, he eased inside her and lost himself in their mutual journey to fulfillment.

As she lay contentedly in his arms afterward, Karen wished they didn't have to move away from each other, not only physically but mentally, as well. Wonderful as their coming together had been, their lovemaking hadn't resolved their differences of opinion. Not that she was angry or annoyed with him—how could she be after what had just happened between them?

Eventually the floor grew uncomfortable and she began to be chilled by a cold draft. Forced out of her daze of happiness by physical discomfort, she suddenly realized that Mrs. Haven might arrive with the crib at any moment. Easing free of Zed's embrace, Karen rose, gathered up her clothes and retreated to the bathroom.

Later, as they walked back to the hospital through the misty afternoon, holding hands, she said, "You seemed preoccupied after you spoke to your sister. Is something wrong?"

"Not with Jade," he said. "There's a problem at the ranch. I've had a long-term grazing agreement with the BLM—the federal government's Bureau of Land Management—which apparently is being revoked without advance notice. When my foreman couldn't locate me, he called Jade and she told me about it."

Her heart sank. "That means you have to return to Nevada."

"As soon as possible. I'll wait for Danny to be discharged and then—"

"If it's an emergency," she interrupted, "you don't have to wait. Go and take care of it. I'm perfectly capable of handling things here."

He frowned at her. "I plan on taking you and Danny back to the ranch with me."

Karen shook her head. "You can't. I mean, I have a job I can't run out on. I've been gone too long as it is."

"Don't you get any time off for Christmas?"

"Naturally, but that's ten days from now. I can't ask the district to keep a substitute in my place all that time. Besides, Danny and I live in San Diego, not in Carson Valley."

"But I thought we'd spend Christmas together at the ranch."

Trying not to react to the tinge of irritation she heard in his voice, she said, "You're welcome to visit us at Christmas."

"Why can't the two of you come to the ranch?"

Why couldn't they? Truth be told, she would like to. On the other hand, it might be best to put some time and distance between them. She needed to slow this headlong rush into a relationship that she feared might break her heart when it ended. Her heart and Danny's, too. He was already attached to Zed.

"Don't you think we need time to sort things out?" she asked. "First of all, the Talal problem isn't resolved and I intend to follow through on that, even if I have to go through our ambassador in Kholi."

"Time?" Zed exclaimed. "Why do we need time? If you want to give anyone time—Talal's the one. Haven't you been listening? I told you he'll be back."

"When pigs fly and hens crow," she snapped, jerking

her hand free of his and halting on the sidewalk to glare at him. "I'm not coming to Nevada, not now, nor at Christmas. All we'd do is argue, anyway."

He half smiled. "That's not all we'd do, and you know it."

Not wanting to admit that was part of the problem— her fear of involving herself too deeply in the relationship—she simply shook her head and resumed walking.

"Stubborn woman," Zed muttered, but she ignored him, trying to hold on to her anger so she wouldn't feel so much pain when they did part.

At the hospital Dr. Nelson hadn't yet been by to see Danny. When he did come, he briefly examined the boy. "Danny looks better every day," he said. "Go ahead and take him home to San Diego, but be sure to have his own doctor follow him for a few weeks. I'll sign his release."

Once the doctor was gone and Karen had busied herself with dressing Danny in clean clothes, Zed said, "We're taking him to Snug Haven for the night. No argument."

Much as she would like to get into the rental car right now and head for San Diego, she knew that wasn't rational. It was already four in the afternoon and she dare not do anything that might harm Danny. Yet she dreaded spending another night with Zed.

"Danny and I may have to stay overnight, but you don't," she told him.

"I'll make my own decisions."

"Just don't base them on the fact there's only one bed in the room," she said tartly.

His scowl darkened his face, giving her the odd sensation she was looking at Talal, not Zed. "I'm perfectly aware Danny will be in the the same room we are." His voice was chilly. "Do you think I can't control myself?"

I don't know, she thought, *but I'm more worried about myself than I am you. How can I sleep with you lying next to me? How can I keep from remembering how wonderful it feels when you kiss me and hold me close?*

Danny, looking from one to the other of them, began to whimper. Zed gave her an angry look and said, speaking between his teeth, "Damn it, I'll see if Mrs. Haven has another room."

As it turned out, she did, and Zed moved into it. As Karen lay alone in the big brass bed that night, instead of being relieved he wasn't there next to her, she felt bereft, as though she'd lost something precious that she might never recover.

Zed, alone in his room, forced himself to concentrate on what his alternatives might be if he couldn't negotiate a compromise with the BLM. Pretty bleak, he decided. Which exactly described his present mood. Bleak.

He'd thought Karen felt as he did, that they were on the edge of something unique, something that deserved more exploration. Apparently he was wrong, because she wanted to end their relationship here and now.

Maybe she was right, maybe they would all be better off. He would see her and Danny safely off in the morning and that would be the end of it. Doing his best not to acknowledge the heavy weight that seemed to have lodged itself in his chest, he told himself that neither Karen nor Danny belonged to him—she was a free agent and Danny was another man's son. Talal's son.

Zed turned over in bed, wishing he could turn away from the puzzle of Talal as easily. How could he be so sure Talal hadn't fled rather than face the situation? The answer came to him as quickly as the question had. *Because I wouldn't do it; therefore, neither would he.*

What kind of an answer was that?

When he woke the next morning and saw the sun was up, he shook his head. The day should be cloudy, should be gloomy, not bright and cheerful. He dressed and knocked on Karen's door. She opened it immediately, inviting him in. Danny, in the crib, raised his arms to be picked up and Zed felt his heart contract as he lifted him.

"Hey, there, Tiger," he said huskily, "I'm going to miss you."

"Da," Danny said, patting his cheek. "Da, da."

Zed took a deep breath and let it out slowly. This was going to be even tougher than he'd imagined. He looked at Karen and saw she was watching them. She turned her head before he could be quite sure whether or not he'd seen tears in her eyes.

It was her choice. She could always change her mind, he told himself. He'd stated his case—he was damned if he meant to plead with her.

Her rental car was parked behind his. By the time he had carried down her luggage and stowed it, numbness had replaced his mixed sadness and anger. He didn't feel anything. Once Danny had been fastened into his new car seat, Zed watched Karen start to slide behind the wheel, hesitate and get out. She took several steps, closing the gap between them.

"Goodbye, Zed," she said.

He'd made up his mind not to touch her or kiss her, but the quiver in her voice undid him. He lifted his hand to her cheek. When he touched her, Karen flung herself at him. His arms went around her automatically, holding her close for a long, poignant moment.

As soon as she made a motion to free herself, he released her and stepped back. Finding goodbye impossible to get out, he swallowed and said, "Good traveling, Karen." Turning away, he slid into his car, where he sat while she pulled from the curb. He didn't start the engine until he could no longer see her car.

Before moving, he punched the steering wheel three times and swore. Because he couldn't vent his frustration against Karen, he muttered, "Damn it, Talal, you'd better prove me right."

As he said the words, a picture formed in his mind, so real he seemed to relive the moment. The red ball arcing up when he threw it. A young boy running to pick it off the sand when it fell. Not Talal, a boy he couldn't put a name to. *"Nisf!"* the boy shouted tauntingly, grabbing the ball and running off with it. With the image still vivid in his mind, Zed suddenly realized that was the word he sometimes said when he was upset. Furthermore, for the first time he knew exactly what *nisf* meant. Half. The boy had insulted him by calling him half.

Zed blinked, shaking his head, orienting himself to the reality of his surroundings. There was no red ball, no sand, no taunting boy. He was parked in front of Snug Haven in Monterey. Shaken, he puzzled over what had happened. A memory, long suppressed?

If he thought about it, the image wasn't as mysterious as it seemed. He'd been born in Los Angeles and moved to Nevada when he was four. Southern California had lots of sand—desert and beach sand—and there were innumerable red balls in the world. A boy of three or four might well remember another kid taking his ball. It all fit except for the word.

. *"Nisf,"* he whispered. He'd bet a bundle that the word was Arabic for half.

What had Talal said? *One, split in two by Allah's will.* Making half.

Chapter Twelve

Zed's first week back at his ranch wasn't too bad. He plunged into the struggle to persuade the BLM to rethink the grazing-rights decision, meeting with other Carson Valley area ranchers, finally hiring a lawyer to represent the coalition they formed. Adding this extra activity to his regular ranch duties kept him tired enough to sleep at night. The problem was, he remembered his dreams when he woke up, and Karen was erotically featured in all of them.

Not until the second week did he begin to have worrisome dreams about Danny being in danger and needing rescue. These seminightmares roused him early in the morning, and he rarely was able to drop back to sleep. The dreams haunted him after he got up and, combined with a lack of sleep, made him jumpy and irritable.

Jade finally took him to task. "Why don't you call

Karen before you lose every friend you ever had? My patience is running low—keep this up and pretty soon you'll have an estranged sister. If you don't call Karen, I will."

"No! This is none of your business."

"Then for heaven's sake, take care of it," she snapped.

Still he held off. With Christmas hovering in the wings he didn't want to hear Karen's voice and know she was hundreds of miles away from him—by her own choice.

Three days before Christmas Jade appeared while he was brooding over his morning coffee, causing a hasty rush to the bedroom to grab his sweatpants.

"I decided you needed an early present," she told him, handing him an envelope tied with a red ribbon. "Stop frowning and thank your kind and generous sister for driving through the snow just to offer you some badly needed preholiday cheer."

"The roads are clear," he observed grumpily, resuming his seat at the table.

Jade raised her eyebrows. "Not up where I live. Is this all the thanks I get for trying to rescue you from what Grandma used to call the dismals?"

"Sorry," he said, meaning it. Jade meant well, and he had no right to dump on her.

She plopped down in a chair across from him and gestured at the envelope he'd set on the table. "Go ahead—open it. I can't stand the suspense."

He untied the ribbon and slid a finger under the envelope flap, lifting it, then shook out the contents, finding, in a packet decorated with ornamented trees and Santa Clauses, the unmistakable tan-and-green oblongs of plane tickets. Glancing at them, he noted his name and the destination. San Diego.

"Well?" Jade asked when he didn't immediately respond. "Where are your cries of joy? Your exclamations of eternal gratitude? I did, after all, provide you with a return trip, too—though it was a close call. The way you've been acting lately, I was tempted to get rid of you permanently by buying only a one-way ticket."

"The flight's Christmas Eve," he said finally.

"Don't think that didn't take some doing! So I refuse to listen to any guff about not using those tickets. Any more complaints and I just may decide to disown you once and for all."

Zed stared down at the tan-and-green oblongs lying on the table in front of him. "It's not a good idea," he muttered.

"Nonsense. It's the best idea I've had so far this year. In case you're going to come up with the excuse that Karen may not be home—forget it. I happen to know she will be."

Zed's head jerked up. "You called her!" he accused.

"Easy, brother mine. Don't get hyper. 'Twas merely a friendly woman-to-woman chat. I didn't even mention your name. All I did was ask how she and Danny were and, in my usual subtle fashion, make sure she wasn't going off somewhere for the holidays."

"You haven't been able to mind your own business since you were old enough to talk," he grumbled.

Jade set her elbows on the table and rested her chin in her hands, her green gaze reminding him of Danny's. "No sister worth her salt sits by and lets her favorite brother go down the tubes," she told him.

"I'm your only brother."

"So far. Am I wrong or did you say Talal might be related to us?"

"Apparently he is." He didn't want to talk about Talal, not even with Jade. "I appreciate the thought behind the tickets, sis, I really do. But if Karen wanted to see me she'd have given some sign of it."

Jade sat back and rolled her eyes. "You can't be serious. If that's true, why did she bother to ask me how you were? And don't tell me she was merely being polite. Not when she bent over backward to make the question seem oh, so casual. Why in God's name are the two of you making yourselves so miserable?"

Zed couldn't hold back his questions any longer. "How is she?" he asked. "How is Danny? I've been having bad dreams about him."

"Karen claims they're both fine, but she did say Danny's been waking up at night and crying—something he hadn't done before unless he was cutting a tooth or had a fever. The doctor assured her there's nothing wrong with him, but she worries about it." Jade eyed Zed levelly. "Personally, my bet is he misses you."

Zed felt as though his heart clenched like a fist in his chest. Could his sister be right? The last thing in the world he wanted to do was to make Danny unhappy.

"I asked Karen to come and live with me," he said. "Her and Danny. She turned me down flat."

"Sweeten the offer," Jade advised, brushing back a lock of hair that had slipped over her eye.

He wasn't about to plead. To anyone. For anything. "I don't get on my knees to anyone," he said stiffly.

"Too bad. If you tried that and said the magic words, it might just work."

He blinked in confusion. *Please* and *thank you* were what Grandma had called the magic words, but Jade obviously wasn't referring to them.

"Never mind, it'll come to you," she said. "Because you're my friend as well as my brother, I sometimes forget men tend to be far more literal minded than women." She sprang up from her chair, came around the table and kissed him on the cheek. "I have to run. I warn you— use the tickets, or else!"

After she was gone he turned the tickets over in his hands. God knows he wanted to see Karen again. And Danny. He couldn't be fonder of the boy if he really was the kid's father. Remembering Danny's word for him— *Da*—he sighed, almost feeling a tiny hand patting his face.

What if I'm wrong and Talal doesn't return? Danny never will have a father. Not unless Karen marries someone.

That scenario didn't appeal to him at all. The thought of Karen in another man's arms and Danny calling that man "Daddy" shook him to the core.

No way. As he made that vow, the penny dropped and he understood exactly what his sister had urged him to do. He hadn't understood what she meant at the time, but now he'd come to the same conclusion on his own.

Rising from his chair, he hiked up his drooping sweatpants and headed for the shower. He had a hell of a lot to do in the next couple of days if he meant to get out of here by Christmas Eve.

In the late afternoon of December 24, under Danny's fascinated gaze, Karen put the last decorative ball on the little spruce tree she'd set up on an end table. She turned on the lights, and when they began blinking on and off he chortled with glee, banging a plastic block against the tray of his high chair.

"Your very first Christmas tree," she said. Unexpectedly, tears came to her eyes and she did her best to blink them back.

What was the matter with her? Lately everything seemed to make her weepy, when she had nothing to cry about. Danny had recovered from his accident and they were together, a family of two, ready to celebrate his first Christmas.

"We'll sing carols," she promised, "but no more Santa Claus, not till you're older."

She'd taken him to one of the malls to see their Santa Claus—a complete fiasco. One look at the white-bearded Santa and Danny had begun to shriek in fright, sobbing all the way through the holiday crowds until they reached the car. It had occurred to her on the drive home that it might have been Santa's beard—he hadn't liked Talal, who wore a beard. Even though one beard was white and the other black, perhaps he associated beards with men he didn't like.

"We don't need anyone, do we?" she asked. "Not when we have each other." As she spoke, her gaze fell on the blue octopus in the playpen and she closed her eyes, knowing she lied.

The doorbell rang. Karen frowned. She wasn't expecting anyone. Two of the women she worked with had invited her to spend Christmas Eve with them and their families, but she'd told both of them she wanted to be alone with Danny for his first one. Who could be at the door? Maybe UPS with a belated package?

She peered through the spy-eye and drew in her breath. It couldn't be! Her fingers seemed to be all thumbs as she fumbled with the lock, finally releasing it. Her heart hammering, she opened the door.

"Da!" Danny cried as Zed walked into the apartment, carrying a large Christmas bag.

"Hello, Karen," he said, setting down the bag.

Restraining her impulse to fling herself into his arms, she smiled and said, "Merry Christmas, Zed."

"Da!" Danny cried again, holding up his arms. "Da, da!" Zed crossed to him, slid the tray out and lifted him from the high chair.

"Hey, Tiger," he said, hugging the boy. "I've missed you."

Danny patted his cheek with enthusiasm. Zed sat down and jogged the boy on his knee, chanting a nursery rhyme about a horse named Dapple Gray.

"I've got a gray pony at the ranch," he told Danny. "You're a tad young at the moment, but pretty soon you'll be riding him. We call him Windy for a reason I won't reveal quite yet." He slanted a glance at Karen and grinned.

What was he talking about? Danny wasn't likely to be at his ranch now or later. But she said nothing. At the moment it was enough that Zed was here.

"There's a pizza in the car," he told her. "I knew you wouldn't be expecting me, so I came prepared. I'd better go and get it before it cools off too much."

When he tried to hand Danny to her the boy clung to him and refused to let go. Zed shrugged. "Okay, Tiger, you can help carry up the pizza," he said, slinging him under one arm. As he opened the door, he said to Karen, "I hope Mrs. Hammond doesn't misconstrue this."

So did she. Lucy, the policewoman, wouldn't be welcome at the moment. She had no intention of sharing Zed with anyone except Danny.

As she helped Zed dig in to the pizza, Karen decided it was the best Christmas Eve supper she'd ever eaten. Afterward, he reached into the Christmas bag, brought out presents for Danny and put them under the tree.

"When does he get to open them?" Zed asked.

"Wait until I put on a Christmas carol CD," she said, "and we'll gather round the tree."

Since the boy insisted on staying glued to Zed, he sat on Zed's lap while she handed him the wrapped packages one by one. Zed did nine-tenths of the unwrapping, allowing Danny to tear some of the paper, which he did with great enjoyment. In fact, he seemed to get more of a kick out of the unwrapping than the actual presents.

Karen looked on, the carols playing softly in the background, and understood what had been missing before. Though single parents could and did raise healthy and happy children, a family really wasn't two, it was three— mother, father and child.

"I'm glad you're here," she said spontaneously. "We both are."

His smile, warm and tender, glowed in his eyes, as well. "I wouldn't want to be anywhere else."

As the evening drew on, Danny began to droop, and Karen tried to take him from Zed to give him a bath and get him ready for bed, but he made it clear that Zed had to come along or he wasn't going. In the end, Zed had to put him into the crib and stand there patting his back and singing carols to him until Danny finally fell asleep.

"At least someone likes my voice," Zed told her when they were back in the living room.

"He's afraid to let go of you in case you disappear again," she said.

Zed shook his head. "I won't." Putting his hands on her shoulders, he eased her down onto the couch. To her total amazement, he proceeded to get down on one knee in front of her. Taking her hand in his, he said, "Marry me, Karen. It's the only solution for us and for Danny."

In her shock, his words jumbled in her head. Marry him? Best for Danny? Yes, he was right. Danny needed a father—specifically, he needed Zed for his father. She must agree, she wanted to agree, she would agree. Gladly. Yet where were the other words, the ones he hadn't said? What about love?

He didn't love her—that's why those words were missing. With tears of both joy and anguish misting her eyes, she chose her words carefully. "We'll marry you, Danny and I. He does need you." *And so do I, more than you'll ever know.*

Rising, Zed sat beside her on the couch and removed a small velvet box from his pocket. He took out a ring and slid it onto her left hand. "I had to guess at the size. It can be made bigger or smaller."

Karen gazed at the diamond nestling among aquamarines in an imaginative gold setting. "It's a perfect fit," she said huskily, tears threatening.

"I chose the aquamarines because of your eyes," he said.

Unable to bear any more—he was being sweet and considerate but what she really needed was his love—she began to cry.

Zed pulled her into his arms, holding her close, murmuring soothingly. Why was she crying? he wondered. Certainly not because she was overwhelmed with joy because he'd asked her to marry him. She'd made it very clear that the only reason she'd agreed was for Danny's sake.

That wasn't exactly why he'd proposed. What he wanted was her. And Danny, too, of course, but Danny was a bonus. Was she upset because she'd said yes?

"I'm s-sorry," she said shakily, easing away to pull a tissue from her pants pocket and wipe her face. "I'm not usually such a weepy-time gal. You probably won't believe me, because I seem to water your shoulder regularly."

"When I start to wear a slicker you'll know it's getting to me," he said, smiling at her. He rose and dug in to the paper bag again, lifting out a bottle of champagne.

"Let's drink a toast to us," he said. "To us and to—" He hesitated and she caught her breath, waiting for his next word. Would it be love?

"To Christmas Eve," he finished.

He opened the bottle with a satisfying pop. She provided two stemmed glasses and he poured the pale bubbling wine into them. While he was pouring, Karen brought in a plate of colorfully decorated Christmas cookies and set them on the low table by the couch.

He raised his glass. "To Karen and Danny," he said, touching her glass.

"And to Zed," she added before taking a sip. She sat on the couch and drank more of her champagne. Glancing at the beautiful engagement ring Zed had given her, she sighed. She'd had a wonderful Christmas Eve and she had just promised to marry the man she loved. Why wasn't she delirious with happiness?

Zed sat down next to her, champagne bottle in his hand. "More wine?" he asked.

She nodded.

He filled her glass and topped his own, then reached for a cookie. Wasn't he even going to seal what she could only think of as their bargain with a kiss? Feeling the beginning of resentment as she watched him munch on the cookie and reach for another, she swallowed more champagne.

Zed knew he didn't dare touch her. One kiss and he would have all her clothes off before she had time to catch her breath. So he drank another glass of wine and ate two more cookies. "These are good," he said belatedly. "Are they homemade?"

She nodded, finished the last drop in her glass and set it on the table. He lifted the bottle to pour more but found the bottle empty.

"When?" she said, folding her arms across her breasts as she sat back.

"When?" he echoed. As she opened her mouth to answer, he decided he knew what she meant. It was about time! He was almost ready to explode.

"When are we going to—?" she began, and got no further. Zed pulled her into his arms, kissing her with all the pent-up need that had been collecting for weeks.

For a fraction of time he thought she meant to resist, but then her lips softened under his, responding to his kiss. They parted, inviting him in, her tongue welcoming his as her hands rose to caress his nape. He slid his hands under her fuzzy red sweater, wanting to touch her skin, wanting to touch her everywhere.

It was as though he'd lit a match and set off a fuse connected to dynamite, Karen thought dazedly as she felt desire rocket through her, fueled by his passionate kisses and intimate caresses. Clothes were in the way, his and hers, she needed to be closer, she could never get close enough to him.

Off came her red sweater, then he unhooked the red bra that matched it and flung the bra aside. He tugged at her black velveteen pants until they came down and off. Her remaining garment was her red-and-black bikini. Meanwhile she finally got all the buttons on his shirt undone and slid it off his shoulders. When the shirt was gone, she unsnapped the band of his pants and reached for the zipper.

"Better let me," he rasped, easing the zipper down. When he yanked the pants off, his shorts went with them and his arousal told her why he'd wanted to be careful with the zipper.

He groaned when her fingers closed around him, but almost immediately he removed her hand. "I want to make it last," he whispered against her lips. His hand, hot through her bikini, cupped her mound, igniting an inner blaze, making her mindless with need.

"Zed," she murmured helplessly, "Please, Zed, please."

He'd been dying to hear those words escape from her lips, was his last coherent thought as he tore off her bikini and plunged inside her, her soft heat surrounding him, giving him a sensual rush, sending him up the steep incline toward release, her undulations and little moaning cries assuring him she was with him all the way.

Much later he shifted her so she lay on top of him, both lazily watching the Christmas tree lights blink randomly. After a time he said, "What was that question you were asking a while back?"

"What question?" she murmured drowsily.

"As I recall, something about when we were going to get around to this. The truth is I was ready the minute I walked in the door, but Danny was still up."

"Oh, that question," she said. "Actually, that wasn't what I meant."

He ran his hand over the curve of her hip. "No? You could have fooled me."

She nuzzled him. "Well, I sort of meant it, but that wasn't what I was asking. It was about the date."

"What date?" As soon as the words were out, he picked up on her meaning. "The wedding, right? How about tomorrow?"

She poked him in the ribs, making him shudder and laugh. "That tickles," he accused.

"You know we can't get married on Christmas Day," she said. "Besides, whether Nevada does or not, California has certain legal requirements. It takes a couple of days. Anyway, I need some time to think about this and to get ready."

"Okay, then, come back with me to Nevada and we'll get married there. Jade can help with whatever arrangements you decide to make."

Her first impulse was to say she couldn't, but then he kissed her and the hot rush of desire burned through her all over again. His slow, tender caresses blanked her mind until nothing existed but Zed and their lovemaking. This time they explored and tasted, in their mutual pleasure delaying the climax while they savored each kiss, each caress, each sensation.

No one had ever made love to her, with her, so completely and wonderfully. The first time had taken the wild edge off their passion, so she could better appreciate and caress him while he discovered all her secret places.

The trip up was slower but no less magic.

Afterward, Karen realized she had no heart to stay behind in San Diego while Zed flew back to Carson Valley. Wherever he was, she wanted to be. Needed to be. Even if he didn't love her.

"All right," she told him, "but I want to plan our wedding, not rush through it. My parents will need time to get to Nevada, for one thing."

Zed sat up, pulling her with him, and grabbed the throw hanging over the back of the couch, wrapping it around them. "I can see this is going to be more complicated than I thought. I sort of had in mind going into one of those little Nevada chapels—there's one up in Tahoe— and getting it over with quickly."

"I don't get married every day! And neither do you. We'll do it right or not at all."

Danny cried out, a frightened cry, sending them both scrambling off the couch. They rushed into the bedroom. When Karen switched on the light, Danny, clutching the bars of his crib rail, stared from her to Zed, his sobs easing.

"Mama," he said, raising his arms. "Dada."

Karen's heart turned over. As she lifted Danny from

the crib, she knew she'd made the right decision. For Danny's sake as well as hers.

Danny was content to be with her for only a moment or two before demanding that Zed take him. After that, he refused to be separated from Zed, setting up a terrible fuss when Zed tried to put him back into his crib.

"No sleeping in bed with us, Tiger," Zed told him. "I'm not about to let you start that bad habit."

"So what do you intend to do?" Karen asked as she slipped into a nightgown.

"Rock him to sleep and then spirit him off to the crib while he's out of it."

"Naked? You, I mean."

"What's wrong with that?"

Karen shrugged. "I guess I can live with it." Actually, she enjoyed watching him walk around without any clothes on. He had a beautiful, masculine body—wide shoulders tapering down to hips that wouldn't hold up sweatpants. She smiled at the thought.

"How about some Christmas music played low?" she asked when he'd settled himself in the chair with Danny in his lap.

"Can't hurt, might help."

"You must have brought clothes with you. Are they at a motel?" she asked after putting on carols.

He shook his head. "In the car. I drove straight here from the airport."

She shot him a mock frown. "Pretty sure I'd ask you to stay here, were you?"

"No, not really." He grinned at her. "Otherwise I'd have brought my bag in with the Christmas stuff and the pizza."

He began to hum "I'm Dreaming of a White Christ-mas," then began to sing it along with Bing Crosby, rock-ing as he sang. Softly, fortunately, because he was off-key. Danny didn't seem to mind, though.

"I'll put on a robe and go down and get your stuff," she offered.

"Thanks. Keys are in my right pants pocket." He told her what make and color the rental car was and where he'd parked it.

By the time she'd got her robe and slippers, located his car and come back to the apartment with his bag, he'd stopped rocking. Zed wasn't singing along to the Christ-mas carols any longer, either. Danny was sound asleep in his lap and Zed's eyes were closed.

"Zed?" she said softly. When he didn't stir she knew he slept. She stared down at the two of them, smiling and shaking her head.

Lifting Danny carefully from his lap, she carried the boy back to his crib without rousing him. Returning to the living room, she arranged the throw over Zed, then brought a blanket and pillow to the couch. She curled up there while the lights of the tree took turns going on and off, watching Zed sleep and listening to the sound of Christmas.

Chapter Thirteen

A week later, at Zed's ranch, Jade and Karen sat at the kitchen table making lists. "I'm up to fifty relatives and guests," Jade said. "Can you think of any more names you'd like to add?"

Karen started to shake her head, then paused. "Wait, don't you think we should invite George Stone and his wife?"

"I'm sure Zed will want to. I'll put them down." After doing so, Jade gave her an assessing look. "You seem kind of out of it. Don't worry, Danny's fine—Zed won't let anything happen to him."

"I'm not worried about Danny," Karen insisted. "I'm sure he's having the time of his life out there in the snow with Zed."

"Then what *is* bugging you? And don't tell me nothing is. You're drooping like a frostbitten plum blossom."

Karen sighed. "I don't know, maybe I'm just tired." Much as she liked Jade, she couldn't confide her secret longing to anyone. Planning her wedding had brought reality to the situation, forcing her to face the problem head-on instead of allowing it to hide in the recesses of her mind.

She really was going to get married in the not-too-distant future, to a man who didn't love her—something she'd sworn she would never do. No, that wasn't quite right. What she and her friends in college had vowed to each other was that they would never marry unless and until they were absolutely sure they were truly in love.

Which she was, even if Zed didn't reciprocate. She couldn't deny he desired her—he was the most fantastic lover a woman could want. But not one word of love crossed his lips. Affection, sweet nothings, but never "I love you." This lack kept her from confessing her love for him. Not only to him but to Jade, as well.

Jade shrugged. "Okay, I'll accept tired, but I don't quite believe that's the entire story. You can be as close-mouthed as Zed."

"You and Zed seem really close."

"Ordinarily we are, but I can't get him to open up about Talal. And you don't talk about Talal, either. Is the subject taboo?"

"Zed and I don't see eye-to-eye about him. But we did have what you might call a conversation about him last night. You remember a couple days ago I showed you the DNA report the lab finally sent me?"

Jade nodded. "Zed and Danny match."

"Yes. So I mentioned to Zed that he and Talal must

have a close DNA match, as well. Do you know what he
said?''

"I can practically hear him saying he didn't care to
discuss it.''

"You're dead right. I got a bit irritated and made a few
snide remarks. 'No wonder you want to avoid the subject,'
I told him. 'It's because you're beginning to realize how
wrong you were about Talal returning and facing his responsibility to Danny.''' Karen made a face. "So then we
started to argue—keeping our voices down so Danny
wouldn't get upset. Do you realize how unsatisfactory it
is to have an argument without once being able to raise
your voice?''

"I can imagine.''

"Mind you, Zed won't admit he's wrong. Talal, he still
claims, will be back. When, I wonder? In time to see
Danny graduate from college?''

"Talal *must* be related to us," Jade said. "That's what
I want to talk to him about. It's fascinating to think we
may have a half brother we never knew existed. If only
our grandparents had told us more about our father.''

"Perhaps they disapproved of him—you know, the no-
man-is-good-enough-for-our-daughter syndrome.''

"I'm dying to meet Talal. You say he actually is the
image of Zed?''

"Except for his beard. For some reason he scared
Danny. Maybe it was the beard, but I prefer to think
Danny somehow sensed he's a creep.''

"You don't really know he is," Jade said.

"Talal may look like Zed but, believe me, he's totally
different from him otherwise. Ordering people around like
some petty potentate!''

"If he's from Kholi, he might just be some kind of a prince," Jade said. "Those Arab countries still have ruling families and all that jazz. Plus, your remark about Talal sending down edicts from above leads me to believe you haven't experienced Zed's takeover complex."

Karen smiled. "He's tried it a time or two."

"It's one of his less endearing qualities, even though he claims I'm worse than he is."

"Talal is more the commanding-general type—like he can't imagine anyone else being in charge—but maybe it's akin to a takeover complex. If you *are* related to him, perhaps it's genetic, as they've discovered being quick-tempered can be."

"Heaven forbid! If that's true, watch out for Danny in a few years." Jade smiled at her. "I'm glad you and Zed worked things out. He can be so stiff-necked at times—the Adams pride—that I was afraid he'd never get around to asking you to marry him."

"We both realized it was best for Danny," Karen said.

Jade frowned. "Yes, of course it is, but—" She broke off and didn't finish whatever she'd started to say. Picking up her list, she said, "Speaking of getting married, if we don't finish this and get off the invitations no one will show up for the wedding."

"Have you ever come close?" Karen asked curiously. "To marriage, I mean."

Jade shook her head. "So far I haven't met a man I'd want to marry. There're lots of nice guys out there, but I'm looking for someone special—and maybe not so nice, you know? I don't mean a brute, just a man who's a tad different than anyone I've ever met."

Karen couldn't help wondering if those "nice guys out

there" wound up letting Jade call all the shots and that was why she'd rejected them as possibilities. Jade *did* have a tendency to take over—if you let her.

"Anyway, I'm too busy digging wells to get serious about anyone," Jade added. "Besides, some men find me intimidating because of what I do. I mean, I had to learn to control the guys on the rigs—drillers are as tough as they come and don't cotton to taking orders from a woman—so I'm not exactly Sweet Sue."

"Not many of us are these days," Karen said.

"True, but some of us are more outspoken than others, and I'm one of those." Jade shrugged. "How did we get onto this subject, anyway? You have a talent for turning the conversation so I wind up talking about me instead of finding out more about my future sister-in-law."

"You already know the stats. The rest is pretty boring, sort of I teach, therefore I am."

Jade shook her head. "Having a cousin drop the responsibility for a newborn in your lap and then setting off to find the kid's father is hardly routine."

"Poor Erin couldn't help dying."

"Of course not. Did your family or hers help at all?"

"Erin's father has never shown any interest in seeing his grandson or helping in any way. My half brother is the only one in my immediate family who wholeheartedly supports what I'm doing. He even sent me money to hire a private detective. The odd thing is that we've never been close—twelve years is quite a gap. I guess I was too much younger to even be a nuisance to him."

Jade checked her list. "Steve Henderson, right? Do you spell his name S-t-e-v-e-n or S-t-e-p-h-e-n?"

"If you asked my father that question he'd say the *ph*

spelling wasn't the Henderson style, give him a *v* any day. I think he meant the plainer the better, but I was never sure. I hope Steve can get away to come to the wedding. I'm not quite sure exactly what he does—something for the government.''

"Married?"

"Divorced."

"Divorce can be so messy," Jade said, "and it's always traumatic. That's one of the reasons I'm not in any hurry to get married. To me, divorce would be an admission of failure. I hate to fail at anything. That's not to say your brother failed," she added hastily.

"I don't know what went wrong with his marriage. If Steve did fail, it's the only thing in his life he ever failed at. Our dad used to say Steve was a success before he was two."

Zed and Danny came in the back door, ending her tête-à-tête with Jade. Danny was beaming and so was Zed, obliterating the slightly sinister look lent by his two-day growth of black stubble.

"Tiger's a regular snow baby," Zed said. "He loved sledding. I can't wait to get him on skis."

Karen was happy to see how securely Zed had bonded with Danny—of course she was. But, somehow, she felt left out. She wasn't jealous of Danny, but neither did she like being treated as Danny's appendage.

"Speaking of skiing," she put in, "I've always preferred cross-country to downhill."

Zed glanced at her. "That's right—you do come from snow country originally. I hadn't thought about it."

Or about me, she told herself.

Jade stayed for lunch but left immediately afterward,

claiming duty called. Danny went down without protest for his nap in his crib, not in the cradle. He'd become too active to be trusted in a cradle.

Since they'd agreed Danny needed his own room, the guest room she'd used before had been changed into a nursery when Karen's belongings arrived from California. Over Zed's protests, Karen had insisted on having her own room, too, furnished with her bed and dresser set from the apartment. Though the room was conveniently located just across the hall from Zed's, it was her own, a place she could go and be private.

"It's all right for now but we'll share the master bedroom once we're married," he'd told her firmly. She'd agreed—after all, marriage was sharing.

But until then she needed her own space. Somehow, since she'd come to the ranch, the lovemaking between her and Zed had changed. She couldn't resist him—passion sizzled on both sides when they came together. Yet, for her, something intangible was missing, something that had been there in the beginning.

Was it because she'd once believed, as she no longer did, that they were falling in love with each other? She loved him; there was no doubt in her mind about her feelings. She would always love him, knowing he didn't love her made a difference, though.

Once she was sure Danny was sleeping soundly, she retreated to her room, closed the blinds and stretched out on her bed, keeping the door open a crack in case Danny woke. She hadn't been sleeping well, so telling Jade she was tired might have been an evasion but it was also the truth. She was more troubled by the coming marriage than she'd admitted to anyone.

She and Danny were alone in the house because Zed had gone out to take care of ranch duties. She would have to learn more about what went on at a ranch, and was, in fact, looking forward to that.

She'd had to give up her teaching position in San Diego when she left. Determined their marriage would be a success, she'd decided to stay home for the rest of the school year to give it every chance. Of course, she was also looking forward to spending extra time with Danny. Maybe next fall she would sign up as a substitute teacher here—she wasn't sure yet. Besides, it was difficult to look that far ahead before she got over the hump of the wedding ceremony.

Propping her head up on a pillow, she picked up the book she'd brought with her and tried to read, but she couldn't concentrate. In any case, the room was too dark with the blinds closed and she didn't have the energy to get up and open them.

She was doing the right thing by marrying Zed—she knew she was, and yet doubts continued to plague her. Karen sighed, put down the book and turned onto her side. Her eyes closed and sleep crept up on her unawares....

Waiting, she lay on her side on a vast heart-shaped bed in a rose-scented bower in a place she didn't recognize. The unfamiliarity didn't bother her because her anticipation ran high. Soon she would know the answer. Soon she would have all her questions answered.

Gradually she became aware she wasn't alone. Someone else lay on the bed behind her. He wasn't touching her or making any sound but, without turning, she knew he was there, knew he was close, knew that he was the one she awaited.

She continued to wait, her anticipation building, until finally his fingers came to rest on her nape, kneading gently, relaxing her tenseness. Soon he was stroking her back soothingly, his hand under her sweater. His touch, though restful, tingled along her nerves, slowly arousing her.

He unhooked her bra, his fingers easing around to cup her bare breast. Though she hadn't meant to allow this, she decided it felt too good to deny. This much and no more.

His hands slipped down under the waistband of her pants to stroke her buttocks. Should she stop him? But how could she when his touch set her aflame?

Soon her pants and bikinis were down around her knees and his explorations included her most sensitive area, causing her to quiver with desire. More, she wanted more, she wished he'd never stop. Yet if he didn't stop she'd go up in flames. And if she did, when she did she wanted him to burn with her, both of them consumed in the fire of their love. He was the one, the right one, the only one she would ever feel such passion for.

He turned her onto her back and eased off her pants. The movement broke her erotic trance enough so she was able to think as well as feel. She knew he was naked and as ready as she was but, though she desperately needed to join with him, she knew she must not. Not until he told her the answer. And to get his answer, she must ask the question.

The words were waiting, had been waiting for oh, so long. So very long. She formed them in her mind and ordered herself to say them, only to discover she couldn't speak. But she must!

Balancing impatiently on the edge of fulfilling her immediate desire, she struggled to force out the question that was so clear in her mind.

"Karen?" he murmured, asking his own question.

Yes, her body urged, yes, yes, as his caresses drove her into a frenzy of need. But how could she tell him yes without hearing his answer to her unspoken question? Why couldn't she ask him if he loved her? Why wouldn't the words come? She made one final, intense try....

Without warning, her eyes opened. To her confusion she found she was in her own bed, though, as in what must have been a dream, naked to the waist. The rest was no dream. He was there in the darkened room, naked, poised over her, waiting, a man who certainly didn't love her.

Still half-asleep, she stared up at him in terror, at the dark beard shadowing his face, and screamed, shoving at his chest with both hands. "No," she cried, scrambling free of him, "get away from me!"

Moments later, fully awake, huddled in the space between her bed and the wall, she gazed uncomprehendingly across the bed at Zed. Glancing quickly around the room, she saw they were alone.

"What's the matter?" he asked.

"I—I thought for a moment you were Talal," she admitted, hugging herself. "It's dark in here and I must have been dreaming."

Zed shook his head. "You scared the hell out of me. I had no idea you were still asleep. When you began to respond to me, I thought you'd woken up." He ran a hand over his stubble. "Guess I'd better shave before we take this any further."

If he meant the lovemaking, Karen had no heart to continue, whether or not he shaved. Still shaken, she was totally out of the mood.

What was wrong with Karen? Zed asked himself that evening after they'd eaten and Danny was in bed for the night. She claimed she felt all right, but she certainly wasn't acting normally. Never before had she turned away when he tried to put his arms around her as he'd done a few minutes ago. All he'd meant to do was kiss her and offer some affection—but she wasn't having any.

He figured it must be tied in with that weird episode earlier when she'd mistaken him for Talal. Damn the man, anyway. Talal was constantly on his mind; he could almost feel his presence. It was as if Talal had claimed a piece of Zed as his own. The feeling unnerved him as much as Talal's continued absence annoyed him.

Not that Danny had to worry. Zed planned to adopt the boy once he and Karen were married—he was sure she would agree it was a good idea. Danny couldn't be any more his son than if he had fathered him. He intended to make it legal as well as emotional.

Could it be Karen was having second thoughts about the marriage? About marrying him for Danny's sake? She'd made it clear enough that was her reason. The words were seared in his mind: *We'll marry you, Danny and I.*

She'd had the sense to see it was the best solution, but he couldn't help wishing she could have found an additional reason for agreeing. He wanted her in his bed every night, wanted her where he could reach out and touch her, but she seemed to be putting that off as long as possible.

The sex continued to be great, as always with her, but he needed more than great sex from Karen.

He envisioned them alone in some isolated spot—say a snowed-in cabin at Tahoe. Without Danny. Maybe Jade could take him for a couple of days. He seemed pretty fond of her. Just Karen and him, together, with no distractions. He found himself getting aroused thinking about it.

Glancing over to where she sat reading, he said, "How'd you like to go cross-country skiing?"

Karen looked up. "Skiing?"

"You said you liked to—so do I. Tahoe is just up the hill, and they have both downhill runs and groomed trails. They've got some great cabins up there. We could leave Danny with Jade and take a few days for ourselves."

Up came that damn thumbnail to her mouth, which meant she was having to think it over. Why should she? In his opinion it was a great idea, offering a way for them to be alone together and maybe ski besides. Obviously she didn't feel for him what he did for her.

"Why don't we wait until after the wedding?" she said. "Danny will have settled in here and be more secure by then, and I'll be more comfortable leaving him with someone else."

"The wedding's not until March thirty-first," he reminded her. "By then we may or may not have good skiing. But at least you're aware we're not taking Danny on our honeymoon." His words were tinged with anger. Couldn't she tell he needed to be alone with her away from the ranch and everything else? Now, not waiting until after the wedding.

She closed her book with a snap. "You don't have to

get ticked off about it. We can cross-country ski in that valley southwest of here—Hope Valley, isn't it? They have groomed trails and it's close enough so we could go and come back the same day. We could even put Danny in a backpack and you could—''

"Damn it!" he grated. "You don't have a clue to what I'm talking about."

"I thought it was cross-country skiing," she snapped.

"How the hell could you mistake me for Talal?" he demanded. "Even in a dream?"

"Is that still bugging you?"

"What do you think? How would you feel if I mistook you for another woman who looked like you?"

"I don't happen to have a twin."

"He's not my twin!" He shouted the denial.

"Shh," she cautioned. "You'll wake Danny."

Zed caught at the tag ends of his anger, taking a deep breath and letting it out slowly. Spacing the words evenly, he said, "Talal can't be my twin. It's impossible."

"Why does the idea infuriate you so? I mean, I can understand why you wouldn't care to have a twin like him, but—''

"There's nothing wrong with the man."

"No? I suppose everyone who acts like he has a divine right to order everyone else around is high on your list of good guys."

"Can't you get it through your head he comes from another culture? He doesn't necessarily react the way we would."

"So because Talal was raised in Kholi, you're saying that makes it all right for him to turn his back on his responsibilities?"

A muscle jumped in Zed's jaw with his effort to keep from shouting again. "I'm wasting my time talking to you," he growled, and stalked off, grabbing his jacket before opening the door and stomping from the house.

Good riddance, Karen told herself angrily as she heard his pickup roar away. At least there wouldn't be any question what bed she slept in tonight. Not that she would have slept with him tonight, anyway. He had to be the most unreasonable man in the entire world.

Is it my fault he came into my room this afternoon and started making love to me while I was asleep? I can't help it if I was confused when I woke up in a darkened room. Nor can I be blamed because he and Talal look so much alike.

Zed hadn't returned by the time she was ready to go to bed. "Who cares?" she asked aloud as she crawled into her own bed, denying how lonely her words sounded and how empty the house felt without him there.

She fell asleep, but woke after several hours and lay listening to the still-not-familiar creaks and groans of the house. The wind had come up and whistled around the outside corners, reminding her of when she was a child in bed at night during New York winters. The sound hadn't bothered her then—rather, she'd felt secure, safe in a warm nest, protected from the windy cold outside.

This house was safe enough, and she was certainly warm under the covers, but now the sound of the wind seemed to mock her. She remembered how her mother, at Steve's wedding, had advised his new bride never to let the sun go down on a quarrel. Who knew if Francine had listened? Or whether following that advice would have prevented the divorce?

I'm certainly not heeding my mother's words, she thought unhappily. The sun is long set.

Glancing at the clock, she noted the time. Nearly three. Rising, she first padded quietly into the nursery, covering Danny, who was sound asleep. Then she approached Zed's ajar bedroom door, hesitating before pushing it open. What could she say to him that might heal the widening breach between them? Uncertain just what she meant to say or do, she pushed open the door and padded slowly toward his bed. Before reaching it, she held.

In the dim light from his open blinds she could see his bedspread had not been turned down. The bed was empty. Zed was not in it.

Telling herself he could have fallen asleep on the couch, she hurried into the living room. He wasn't there. Nor was he anywhere else in the house.

At three o'clock in the morning Zed still hadn't come home.

Chapter Fourteen

The next weekend Jade came to the ranch with a long string of wedding arrangements for Karen to okay. Since she was getting married in Nevada rather than at their home in New York, Karen's parents were asking her to make all the arrangements, while insisting they would foot the bill. Though grateful for their generosity, Karen felt guilty because she couldn't work up a proper enthusiasm for the preparations.

Halfway through Jade's explanations, Karen sighed and said, "I wish it was all over."

"I don't blame you," Jade told her. "This setting-up stuff is a pain."

"It's not so much the arrangements. I mean, you're doing most of the work. It's just that—" She broke off and sighed again.

Jade raised her eyebrows. "I take that to mean you and my brother haven't forgiven and forgotten."

"Are you talking about that night he lit out like a wounded bear and didn't come back until God only knows when?" She'd told Jade about the quarrel without revealing its exact cause, expecting that Zed already had talked about it. She'd been wrong. Zed hadn't confided in his sister.

"That night and whatever else is making you so jumpy around each other," Jade said.

"It was only an argument. There was nothing to forgive," Karen said. "Not really. Even if he never did tell me where he was until way after three."

"I can make a pretty good guess. One of his high school buddies inherited Lucky Joe's Casino just outside Genoa. My bet is he was in there hoisting a few with J.J.—Joe Junior. J.J.'s on the guest list, by the way. And what do you mean, there was nothing to forgive? If two people have a fight there's always something to be forgiven—usually on both sides."

Karen couldn't bring herself to tell Jade what the real problem was. Ever since the night they'd argued, Zed hadn't once tried to make love to her, hadn't indicated by word or gesture that she'd be welcome in his bed, hadn't even kissed her good-night.

"We were arguing about Talal again," she said finally, which was partly the truth.

"Give it up," Jade advised. "Either Talal will show again or he won't. Why argue about it?"

Danny, sitting at the end of the table in his high chair, flung his plastic bell-ball off the tray, following it down with his gaze until it hit the floor with a loud tinkle. He chortled and then looked expectantly at Jade. "Te," he said.

"We're playing the auntie-will-pick-it-up-so-you-can-throw-it-down-again game, are we?" Jade asked him.

"The baby book says he's doing it because he's learned a new skill, but he learned that particular one over a month ago. I keep hoping it will pass," Karen said.

"Pass it will, probably into another phase that'll drive us all nuts before he gets tired of it," Jade said, picking up the toy and holding it. "It's a good thing you're such a cute little guy that none of us can resist you," she told Danny.

"Te!" he exclaimed, reaching toward her, obviously demanding she hand him the ball.

Jade shook her head in resignation and complied. Karen hid a smile when the toy promptly hit the floor again. The back door opened and Zed came in, wiping the dirt off his boots onto the mat. The snow had melted and mud was everywhere.

"Da!" Danny said, his attention now focused on Zed.

"Good," Jade said. "Let Da play with you for a while. He just loves to pick toys up from the floor."

Zed shucked off his jacket and lifted Danny from the high chair. "Driving the girls crazy, are you, Tiger?" he said. "Nothing like getting a head start."

Shifting the boy onto his hip, he plucked a mug from the tree and headed for the coffeepot. Before he got there he held, his head cocked as though listening. "We expecting anyone?" he asked.

Karen then heard the muted roar of an engine—Zed had the most acute hearing of anyone she'd ever met. "Not that I know of,'' she said, rising. ''Go ahead, have your coffee. I'll see who it is.''

''Sports car,'' he said. ''Dual pipes. I'll bet on foreign. Could be J.J. I'll take care of it.''

Karen sank back down and he left the kitchen.

''So,'' Jade said, picking up one of the cards she'd brought with her, ''do you want to go with this bakery for the cake or not?''

''Why not?'' Karen said. ''They sound fine. Maybe you should run the flower arrangements past me again. I wasn't paying close attention the first time. I know I definitely do *not* want gladiolas—or is it gladioli? I never can remember.''

Jade shuffled through the papers she'd brought, muttering, ''Flowers, flowers, I know you're in here somewhere. Ah, there you are. The florist suggested white and pink as the color scheme, with some blue sprinkled in, honoring the 'something blue' superstition, I guess. They said—'' She broke off to stare as Zed reentered the kitchen.

Her blank expression made Karen turn to look. She gasped and got up hastily.

''You remember Karen,'' Zed said to the man with him, a man with a walking cast on his left leg, supporting himself with a cane. ''Jade, this is Talal Zohir, Danny's father.''

''My God,'' Jade muttered, obviously completely taken aback.

Karen didn't blame her. This was Jade's first glimpse. Since the last time Karen had seen him, though, he'd shaved off his beard so that now he was the exact image of Zed. Danny, in Zed's arms, stared at Talal with his mouth open.

"I'm happy to see you again, Karen," Talal said. "Jaida, I'm very pleased to meet you, my sister."

Jade stood and raised her chin. "It's Jade," she said, "not Jaida."

Talal nodded. "I used the Arabic name. If it troubles you, I'll try to remember to call you by the American variant."

"Why did you call me sister?" Jade demanded.

"Shall we go into the living room?" Karen asked, trying to play the polite hostess as she coped with her shock—she'd never expected to see Talal again—as well as an impending sense of doom.

"By all means," Zed said. "We'll sit down where it's comfortable. Talal looks like he needs to get off that leg."

The situation didn't seem quite real to Zed—Talal in his house—even though he'd been confident of Talal's return. "Coffee?" he asked as they trailed into the living room.

"None for me," Talal said. Jade and Karen shook their heads.

I could use some, Zed thought, but gave up the idea in favor of sitting down to hear what Talal had to say.

"You haven't answered my question," Jade said to Talal as soon as they all were seated.

"I'll do so shortly," he told her. "Karen, if you would be so kind as to bring me a small stool to rest my leg on?" After she fetched an ottoman from the den, he thanked her, adding, "Ah, that's much better," as he propped the casted leg up on the stool.

Talal looked from one to the other of them, ending with

Jade. "You are my sister," he said, "for the same reason that Zeid is my twin. Because we share the same parents—the same mother, Ellen Adams, the same father, Shas Zohir."

"Twins!" Zed exclaimed. "But—"

"I anticipated your objection," Talal said. "I was not born in Kholi as I had always been told, as, in fact, my birth certificate states. My birthplace was Los Angeles, California. I was the firstborn of twin boys. You were the second born, Zeid. I have also unearthed long-hidden photographs that show us together."

Astounding as the news was, Zed accepted Talal's words as true without asking to see the photos. "How did you learn this?" he asked.

"In good time, my brother." Talal leaned forward, gazing intently at Danny. "Hello, son," he said softly. Reaching into a pocket, he extracted a red rubber ball, somewhat the worse for wear. "This was once Uncle Zeid's," he said, tossing the ball to Zed.

Holding the ball in one hand, Zed stared at it, aware this was the red ball from his memory. Danny poked a finger at the ball, drew it back and resumed his study of Talal.

"I apologize for leaving so abruptly when I was in the Monterey hospital," Talal said. "Until I forced the truth from my—our—grandmother, I could not make any arrangements for the boy. I had to get at the truth before anything else was done. Now that I have, I've returned to take care of what I must do. In view of the blood typing, I have no doubt Danny is my son, but, of course, I must make absolutely certain, because the authorities will demand proof."

"The authorities?" Zed repeated, not quite certain what Talal was driving at.

Talal shrugged. "All governments tangle themselves in red tape, yours as well as mine. I'll have to prove to both that Danny is my son before I arrange to bring him home to Kholi."

Zed stiffened, feeling Talal's words stab into his heart. "No!" he cried, clutching the boy to him. "You can't take Danny! Absolutely not!"

"But he is my son," Talal said, his voice calm. "Of course I intend to raise him. After all, he is a Zohir. He is a part of our royal family."

"You can't take him," Zed repeated. "He belongs with us, with Karen and me."

Danny began to whimper. Karen sprang up and hurried to him, saying to Zed, "Please let me take him."

Realizing his tight hold on the boy and his angry voice might be frightening Danny, Zed reluctantly gave him to Karen, who resumed her seat, cradling the boy protectively.

"What's this about a royal family?" Jade asked, pushing a strand of hair away from her eye.

"The Zohirs are Kholi's ruling family," Talal said. "You didn't know?"

"I'm not an expert on the Middle East," she said. "And my name is *not* Zohir."

"It is," Talal corrected. "Though born posthumously, you are the legitimate daughter of Shas Zohir. In Kholi you would be addressed as Princess Jaida."

"Let's hear the entire story," Zed said grimly.

Removing a packet from his jacket pocket, Talal took out two photographs, extending them toward Zed. "If you will be so kind," he said, gesturing toward his leg as if in apology.

Zed rose and took the pictures. In the first he recognized his mother standing next to a handsome man with dark hair and beard. Each held the hand of a small boy, boys exactly the same in size and appearance. One of the boys was him, he knew, from the similarity to photos his grandparents had taken of him when he was small. The other boy had to be Talal. In the second his mother was alone, sitting in a chair with her two little boys flanking her. She appeared to be pregnant.

"Those were taken at our grandparents' home," Talal put in. "Our mother lived with them after our father was killed. That is, she lived with them until she managed to escape from Kholi and return to America."

"Escape?" Zed echoed, his attention diverted from the pictures. Seeing Jade gesturing at him impatiently, he crossed the room and handed her the photos.

"Our mother was free to leave at any time—but without us. Our grandfather was reluctant to give up his grandsons, the only ones he had, to have them raised in a foreign country, not as proper Arabs. I can understand his feelings, whether or not I approve of what he did. Grandmother, as his wife, naturally agreed with him."

Talal made an odd gesture, touching his head with his hand, as though seeking to adjust something that wasn't there. He frowned briefly and went on. "Our grandfather no longer lives. I doubt he would ever have admitted the truth. This is what our grandmother, under some pressure from me, finally told me. Our mother, unhappy in Kholi and determined to get away before she delivered another child to be held as a hostage, found a way to escape with us. At the last moment her plans went awry and, though she managed to bring you with her, I had to be left behind or she would have risked being caught and stopped.

"You and I were born prematurely when our mother made a trip to California to visit her parents some three years previously. Once we weighed enough to leave the hospital, our father promptly returned all three of us to Kholi. So my grandfather Zohir worried that our mother might somehow be able to claim me, since I was American born. In order to protect against this, he had his brother, Kholi's ruler, intervene to alter my birth certificate to show I was Kholi born. It was also agreed I would never be told the truth, never be told I had a twin."

"I was never told, either," Zed admitted, staring down at Talal. "I never knew."

Talal nodded. "In a way, I can understand. Our Adams grandparents seem to have been as frightened as our Zohir grandparents. Before she died our mother must have convinced them you and Jaida might be kidnapped and taken to Kholi. I've done some research in California and I discovered they had your last name changed to Adams on your birth certificates."

So that explained the move to Nevada, Zed thought. To make it more difficult for anyone from Kholi to find them. He'd wondered why his grandfather had started his Carson City drilling business at a relatively advanced age.

"You understand that, as Zohirs," Talal continued, "you and Jaida are entitled to recognition as part of the Kholi royal family." Talal grinned at him. "Prince Zeid."

Dazed by all he'd heard, stunned to find Talal was his twin, Zed shook his head. He had no desire to be a Kholi prince.

"You and Jaida also have a legitimate claim to our father's properties in Kholi," Talal went on. "As you may have deduced, the Zohirs are a wealthy family. Money will never be a problem for Danny."

"You can't take him!" Karen cried suddenly. "If you try, it will be over my dead body!"

Jade glared at Talal. "What kind of a brother are you? A rotten one, that's what. How dare you walk in here and break everyone's heart? You're not only trying to snatch Danny from those who love him but you've disrupted Zed and Karen's wedding plans."

Talal, after shifting his gaze from Karen to Jade, settled on Zed. "I had no intention to cause trouble."

"I wish I'd never found you," Karen said to Talal, her voice high and tight with what Zed knew was anguish. "Zed's more of a father to Danny than you could ever be!"

"Karen's raised Danny from the beginning," Jade put in, practically shouting at Talal. "How can you take him away from the only mother he's ever known? Who wants a brother like you!"

Danny began to wail, obviously upset by all the raised voices. His crying roused Zed from his bemusement. Crossing to Karen, now standing, he put an arm around her shoulders and spoke to Danny.

"Hey, Tiger, it's okay," he said softly. "Nothing's going to happen. You're safe with us."

When Danny's sobbing eased, Zed turned to face Talal. Unlike Karen and Jade, Zed felt his anger toward his twin abating. He might fight him to the last to prevent him from gaining custody of Danny, but at the same time he understood exactly where Talal was coming from. He knew what motivated him.

What his twin wanted to do was exactly what he'd wish to do under the same circumstances. He'd unknowingly sired a son and, now that he'd found out about the boy, he wanted to raise him. What Talal didn't realize was how devastating taking Danny away from Karen would be both to her and the boy. He was damned if he meant to allow his twin to hurt either of them.

Watching Talal struggle to his feet, he tried to put words together that might convince him to change his mind.

Before he could speak, Talal said, "Apparently I've plunged your household into turmoil. It's clear I've outstayed my welcome. Will you be kind enough to walk me to my car?"

Zed nodded. After giving Karen a reassuring pat, he saw his brother out the door and over to the red sports car parked in front. A foreign job, exactly as he'd thought.

"Some attention grabber," he told Talal. "It's a beaut. I'll bet it's also a ticket attracter."

"Pardon?" Talal said.

"We have a theory in Nevada that red cars attract more speeding tickets than any other color."

"Oh?"

"Look, we have to talk," Zed said. "How about giving me a lift to Lucky Joe's in that cop magnet of yours? I could use a beer. How about you?" As soon as the words were out, Zed remembered most Arabs didn't drink alcohol. "Sorry," he added. "I forgot you're probably a Muslim."

"In Kholi I abide by their laws. Here in your country,

I abide by yours. I learned to enjoy an occasional beer when I was at Princeton. Lucky Joe's it is.''

On the way to the casino they limited their conversation, avoiding controversy. First they spoke about the car's performance. ''She runs like a scalded cat,'' Zed observed admiringly as they zipped around a dawdling car.

Talal smiled. ''You Nevadans have a unique way of expressing yourselves. Quite different from those who live on the East Coast.''

''Yeah, we're Westerners—a dying breed, I'm afraid.''

''Jaida seems very much a Western woman.''

Zed nodded. ''Which reminds me. Do you have any idea why my—our—Adams grandparents had a cradle that apparently came from the Zohir family? Jade slept in it as a baby and they always called it her cradle.''

''I do know, because Grandmother Zohir mentioned the 'missing cradle' from time to time. Apparently our father ordered it sent to the States when he realized our mother was going to deliver us in Los Angeles rather than waiting until they returned to Kholi. The cradle took so long to arrive in California that the four of us were back in Kholi before it got there. Evidently the Adamses kept the cradle and, as you say, used it for Jade. You and I never slept in that cradle.''

They drove on in silence until Talal said, ''Americans are fond of what they call middle names. Does Jaida have one?''

''Jade Ellen,'' Zed told him. ''Our mother's name. Mine is Zed William, after Grandpa Adams. What's yours?''

''Talal Shane. I often wondered why.''

"Erin must have known your middle name."

"She could have," Talal said. "I may have told her. I don't remember. Why?"

"Because Shane is also Danny's middle name. Our mother must have chosen Shane for you because of it being Grandma Adams's maiden name."

They were nearing the casino, so he pointed it out, telling Talal where the best parking was. Inside, J.J. was nowhere to be seen. Zed led his brother past the rows of brightly lit gaming machines to a small bar tucked away in a corner. In deference to Talal's bum leg, he indicated a small table flanked by two chairs rather than choosing a bar stool. Other than the bartender and one man sitting at the bar, they were the only patrons.

"Anything special you prefer?" he asked.

"I prefer American to foreign—any brand, draft if possible."

Zed brought back two foam-topped glasses, sat down across from his brother and said flatly, "I won't let you take Danny away from Karen, not while he's a child. Let's start from there."

"I'm his father."

"Granted. No one denies that. But—"

Talal held up his hand. "Permit me to tell you a story. I am a widower. My wife was very carefully chosen for me by my—our— grandfather while I was still a boy and she a girl. Since he was old-fashioned and since I was largely educated in the United States and therefore not home much after I reached my teens, my fiancée and I didn't meet until shortly before our wedding."

"I'm surprised Grandfather Zohir permitted you to come to the States."

"His brother, Kholi's ruler, decided where I was to go to school. Because I had a talent for languages, he told my grandfather that I was to be groomed as a family liaison between the Zohirs and the U.S. In order to best prepare me to take on this position, he ordered Grandfather to send me to America for my education. In our country, even a brother hesitates to question the ruler's decree.

"I returned to Kholi after my graduation from Princeton and married my chosen bride. She was a pretty girl and, though I was not in love with her, I found the marriage satisfactory. Unfortunately, she became jealous, suspecting me of lusting after every woman I saw.

"When she became pregnant I hoped her unreasonable jealousy would abate, and it did seem to. We got along quite well until near her time to have the child, when she was told by a tattling troublemaker in the family that I had been seen with a beautiful foreign woman who flaunted her body in public places. You understand that, in Kholi, our women still wear the traditional dress and veil when outside the home."

"So I've heard," Zed said, careful not to sound disapproving. His father might have been an Arab, but Kholi's culture wasn't his and he actually knew very little about the country.

"Instead of confronting me with this ridiculous gossip—I had been, by order, escorting the French ambassador's daughter to various functions—my wife took it to heart. In a frenzy of jealousy she decided to punish me by running off to her Bedouin relatives so the baby wouldn't be born under my roof. Foolishly, she took no one except her personal attendant with her. My wife, like other Kholi women, had never learned to drive, but her maid, being a Bedouin, knew how to handle the four-wheel-drive van. Neither woman paid any attention to the weather and they were caught in a sandstorm before reaching the Bedouin camp. All three died.''

"Three?'' Zed asked, momentarily confused.

Talal took a long swallow of his beer. "My son was born sometime during the storm. He did not survive.''

"My God!'' Zed exclaimed. He reached across and briefly gripped his brother's shoulder in lieu of finding the right words to convey his sympathy.

"That happened three years ago,'' Talal said. "I doubt I will ever marry again, though I've been pressured by the family to continue the line. Now, suddenly, Allah has provided me with a son I didn't know I'd sired.'' He held Zed's gaze. "A son you don't want me to raise.''

What a hell of a dilemma, Zed thought, his heart going out to his brother. Talal needs Danny—but so does Karen. After weighing all the considerations, he finished his beer, setting the glass down with a clunk. "The important one in this is Danny himself,'' he observed. "We need to decide what's best for him.''

Talal didn't respond immediately. The bartender walked over and set two more glasses of beer in front of them. "On J.J.,'' he said, picking up the empty glasses.

"Tell him thanks,'' Zed responded.

Talal turned his glass slowly around, looking at the head of foam instead of at Zed. For the first time Zed noticed that he used his right hand, not his left, and he commented on it, mentioning that he was a lefty.

"Yes, I'm right-handed,'' Talal agreed. "I've heard it's often that way with twins—one right and one left.'' He took a swallow of beer and finally looked at Zed.

"I never forgot you," he said so softly Zed had to strain to hear him. "No matter what they told me, I knew Zeid existed. What I believe is that, though I can't recall it, I saw our mother take you away, leaving me behind."

Zed related the only memory he had, of the red ball and the yellow ball and a boy jeering that he was only half.

"I remember the balls, but I don't recall the incident," Talal said. "The boy was probably Malik. He's several years older than we are. That must have been about the time his father took him into the desert to be raised for the next five years by his Bedouin relatives. You might call it returning to his roots. As I'd like to do with Danny."

"He's still a baby—he needs his mother. To Danny, his mother is Karen."

"I can see that is true. She seems to be a much different type of woman than Erin. Her cousin, you said?"

Zed nodded. "Karen is a wonderful mother. She's wonderful, period."

"Our sister said you and Karen had set a wedding date." Talal's smile held a hint of sadness. "Yours is obviously a love match."

Zed shrugged. "She's marrying me so Danny will have a father figure in his life."

Talal frowned. "But you love her?"

"Can't help myself." Zed smiled wryly. "You've heard of fool's gold—pyrite? It glitters and shines and the unwary believe they've found a fortune. Gold gleams, too, but it's the real thing. I never knew Erin, but that's how I perceive the two of them—Erin as pyrite and Karen as true gold."

"I'm ashamed to say I scarcely remember Erin, though I know we had fun sailing together. She was no more than a passing fling. I was certain I was the same to her."

"From what Karen has told me," Zed said, "you're probably right about Erin's feelings for you. A passing fling about sums it up."

"Yet she bore my son, and for that I'm eternally grateful to her. Allah chooses odd pathways to reward us. You must know I can never give up Danny. He is *my* son. But you've opened my eyes to the other issues at stake. Grant me a few days to think about what is right for all of us—for you and me, for Danny and for Karen."

When they left the casino, both stood for a moment blinking in the bright sunlight, then they walked to Talal's car, Zed slowing his pace to match his brother's.

"Your ankle and leg healing okay?" he asked.

Talal nodded. "The doctors say the worst possible complication may be a slight permanent limp. My poor *Maddamti* is a total loss, though. I was very fond of her."

"I'll have to take you out on my sailboat. You ever been on Tahoe?"

"The lake in the Sierras? No, I haven't."

"That's where we'll go as soon as the weather warms up." His enthusiasm abated as he remembered Talal might not be here that long. "Brother," he said, testing the word. "I can't get used to having a twin brother." He clamped a hand on Talal's shoulder. "I hardly know you and yet I know you well."

"In Kholi, brother, men are not afraid to show affection for one another." He put his arms around Zed, hugging him.

Zed stiffened for an instant, then hugged Talal in return,

the gesture warming his heart. When they broke apart he found himself blinking back tears.

"As I told you once before, Allah took one and split it in two. We are, as Malik once taunted you, each half of a whole. We know each other in a way no one else will ever understand. Believe me when I say I will work something out with Danny that we both can live with. We and your Karen, too. Maybe even our sister—what a feisty one she is. Zohir women are notoriously hard to handle."

After Talal dropped him off at the ranch and drove away, Zed walked slowly toward the house, his mind in a turmoil, his loyalties stretched in too many different directions. Neither Karen nor Jade would understand his feelings, because they viewed Talal as the enemy.

They were wrong. Talal needed Danny and he also had a right to him. In a way, he was on Talal's side because he felt what Talal must be feeling. And yet he knew that if he had to, he'd fight his newfound twin to keep Danny with Karen, fight him to the bitter end.

Chapter Fifteen

The next morning Zed rose early and put on his sweatpants in deference to Karen—he would avoid running around naked at least until they were married. If the wedding was still on. From the cool reception he'd gotten from her on his return from Lucky Joe's, he wasn't sure.

He was pouring his first cup of coffee when she shouted at him. "Zed! Come here quick!"

Alarmed, he raced into the hall, calling, "Where are you?"

"In Danny's room."

He dashed into the nursery and stopped short. Danny, on his hands and knees on the floor, inched slowly ahead.

"He's actually crawling!" Karen exclaimed. "I put him down to strip off the damp crib sheets and away he went, just as though he'd been doing it all his life."

Zed gazed down at the boy, who was so intent on perfecting his newfound skill that he paid no attention to either of them. He grinned at Karen and she smiled back at him, momentarily united as they shared their pleasure at this milestone in Danny's life.

"I predict we're really in for trouble now that he's mobile," Zed remarked.

Karen's smile faded. "What if we never get to see him take his first step? We won't if Talal has his way."

"Talal's not a monster," Zed declared. "Give him some time to think things through."

Karen frowned. "Sometimes I almost believe you're on his side. He may look like you, but that doesn't mean he thinks or acts like you. He's already told us exactly what he intends to do—take Danny to Kholi."

"If he holds to that," Zed observed, "the legal process will take time, giving us a chance to counter his move."

"Unless he decides to bypass legalities and kidnap Danny."

Zed scowled at her. "Talal would never do such a thing!"

"How do you know?" Karen cried. "Twin brother or not, you've barely met the man."

"I know because he *is* my twin. He's me, or almost."

Karen shook her head. "I can't buy that."

Danny reached the rocker and stopped, seeming to ponder his next move. He turned his head and looked at Zed. "Dada!" he ordered.

"You don't suppose he expects me to move the rocker, do you?" Zed asked, relieved at the distraction. Arguing with Karen about Talal got him nowhere.

"I'd say at the very least he's counting on you to solve the problem," she said.

"Okay, Tiger, here goes." Zed dropped to his hands and knees beside Danny. "You've got to learn to go around things," he told the boy. "You can't always count on someone to move obstacles for you. If you can't go around, retreat isn't necessarily failure. And there's always the possibility you can change negative into positive. We'll start with going around."

As Karen watched Zed slowly maneuvering on his hands and knees, obviously hoping Danny would imitate his movements and turn, her annoyance faded. How could she stay mad at a man who loved Danny so much? She didn't understand how he could be so blind where his twin was concerned, though—didn't he recognize the threat posed by Talal? Arguing about it didn't help. She was wasting her breath; she might as well let it go. At least for the moment.

Danny seemed to enjoy Zed's performance but didn't copy the crawling turn, even after several demonstrations. Finally Zed turned toward the rocker, easing up onto his knees. Lifting and supporting Danny, he stood him on his feet and placed Danny's hands on the rocker seat. "Positive, not negative, right?" he said, gradually removing his support until Danny stood by himself, holding on to the rocker.

Danny's stance didn't last long; he plopped down onto his butt and positioned himself on his hands and knees, now facing Karen, and began to crawl again.

"Way to go, Tiger," Zed said, standing and hitching up his sweats. "Never give up until you try all the alternatives."

Marring Karen's enjoyment of the interaction between the two of them and her pleasure at Danny's new skill was her fear of what Talal meant to do. Why hadn't she left well enough alone? Why had she ever begun the search for Danny's father to begin with? If she hadn't, she wouldn't be facing the threat of losing the boy.

Of course, she wouldn't have met Zed, either, wouldn't have discovered the joy of loving. Or the pain.

Jade came by in the early afternoon, still simmering over what she referred to as Talal's "attitude." Pacing up and down in the living room, she waved her hands in the air as she raved on. "Who does he think he is, anyway? Dropping in from nowhere and behaving like he possesses some divine right."

"Maybe it comes from being a prince in his country," Zed observed mildly.

Jade nodded. "Good point. Princes have power and power always corrupts." She fixed her gaze on Zed. "You did little, brother mine, to help matters by roaring off to Lucky Joe's with him. Talk about fraternizing with the enemy."

"He's our long-lost brother, sis."

"Relatives make the worst kind of enemies," Jade said. "I wish he'd stayed lost."

"We all do," Karen put in.

Zed shook his head. "I don't agree. Through Talal, Jade and I discovered who our father was and learned about the deceit both sets of grandparents practiced through fear. Danny will grow up knowing who his father is—more important than you can imagine."

"If Danny had to pick," Jade said, "I'm sure he'd choose you as his father rather than Talal. Didn't you notice how he stared at Talal yesterday?"

"Rather than being afraid of him, I think he was puzzled because Talal and I look alike," Zed answered.

Karen, who was gazing out the window, said, "Speak of the devil."

Zed heard the engine and glanced to the window in time to see Talal's red car pull to a stop in front of the house. As he strode from the room to open the door, he heard Jade mutter, "Enter the villain."

Standing in the open doorway watching Talal lurch toward the house on his walking cast, Zed couldn't help but wonder how different both his life and Talal's might have been if they'd known, as they grew up, of each other's existence.

Since he'd met his twin, he hadn't suffered through his dream of searching through endless fog, making him believe Talal was what he'd unknowingly been looking for all along. But he couldn't fault his grandparents—they'd been sure what they did was the best for all concerned. It still blew his mind to realize he had relatives in Kholi. His Grandmother Zohir was an unknown quantity, so he was unwilling to pass judgment on her, though he had a hunch he wouldn't have cared much for Grandfather Zohir.

"*Marhaba!*" Talal exclaimed.

Deciding this was an Arabic greeting, Zed said, "Hello to you, too. Come on in."

"Are you so certain, then, I'll do the right thing?" Talal asked.

"You're welcome in my home under any circumstances," Zed assured him. "Which doesn't mean I'll always agree with you." He gestured toward the living room. "Karen and Jade are in there."

"And the boy?"

"Taking a nap."

Jade, still standing, took a step toward Talal as he entered the living room. Seeing she was about to burst into impassioned speech, Zed said firmly, "Sit down, sis. We need to listen to Talal, not to you."

She subsided into a chair, scowling.

Zed indicated a chair for Talal but his brother shook his head, so Zed also remained standing, one foot on the raised hearth. Karen, on the couch, hugged herself as she eyed Talal uneasily.

Bracing himself with his cane, Talal glanced from one to another of them and said, "I've come to see my decision was not the best one to be made. It won't work. Do not mistake me—I have every intention of following through on my plans to legally prove that Danny is my son. But I've changed my mind about taking him to Kholi."

He shifted position, his gaze meeting Zed's for a long moment, then traveling to Karen. "My brother and I talked this over yesterday at Lucky Joe's. After we parted company, it became clear to me there's no reason I can't share custody of my son with the two people who mean the most to little Danny—Karen and Zeid." He smiled at Karen, who offered him an uncertain smile in return.

"What do you mean by share?" she asked.

"The two of you are in love," Talal replied, "and soon will marry. My position involves much travel and it's obvious you two, a loving couple, will give Danny a far more stable, caring home than I can provide at present. My son couldn't be in better hands than he'll be with you two raising him. I will, of course, take him to visit Kholi when he's older and can understand he belongs to two countries. In the meantime Zed will be Daddy Z and I will be Daddy T. In time, as he matures, he'll be told the truth. I hope the three of you will visit Kholi when Danny does."

Striding to his brother, Zed reached for his hand. Talal drew him closer and hugged him. For a long moment they stood clasped in each other's embrace, then Zed stepped back. Clearing his emotion-clogged throat, he choked out, "Thank you from the bottom of my heart."

Karen, hovering, eased between them to give Talal a hug and a quick peck on the cheek. "I misjudged you," she murmured. "I should have known Zed's twin had to be one of the good guys." Wiping at her damp eyes with the back of her hand, she said, "I need a tissue," and left the room.

Jade hadn't moved. Since she was seated far enough away that she couldn't overhear, Zed saw his chance to set his brother straight. Keeping his voice low, he said, "You're right about Karen and I getting married, but it's not a love match on her side. It's purely for Danny's sake. Don't you remember me telling you that yesterday?"

"I know you told me *you* love *her,*" Talal said. "Have you ever said those words to Karen?"

Zed shook his head. "What good would it do?"

"Zohirs have an overabundance of pride, but none of us are fools. Swallow your pride. Tell her."

At that moment Karen reentered the room.

"Now!" Talal ordered, raising his voice so that both Karen and Jade couldn't help but hear him. "In front of witnesses."

Embarrassed by his brother's insistence, not seeing an

easy way out and suddenly feeling maybe he hadn't put it quite right the first time, Zed crossed to Karen and took both her hands in his.

"Karen," he said. "I love you. Will you marry me?"

She stared blankly at him, speechless for endless moments.

"Karen," Talal prompted, "it's your turn."

Flinging her arms around Zed's neck, she cried, "I love you with all my heart. I'd never consider marrying any other man."

Oblivious of anyone but Karen, Zed kissed her, long and thoroughly, hardly hearing the plaintive voice from the nursery.

"Dada!" Danny cried.

"Don't move," Jade said. "I'll get him."

Zed released Karen, keeping his arm around her waist as he watched Jade return carrying Danny. Instead of coming to him, she walked directly to Talal. Danny gazed at Talal. "Da?" he said, doubt in his voice.

"Hello, *Nimr*," Talal said gently. "Don't be confused. You're Tiger to Zeid and *Nimr* to me, one and the same word in different languages. Soon you'll learn you have two different fathers who, in a way, are also the same."

Danny twisted in Jade's arms, searching until he saw Zed. "Dada!" he cried.

Jade handed him over to Zed and marched up to Talal again. She smiled at him and said, "Adamses have their pride, too, so I got a double dose. I've never liked admitting I was wrong but, just for you, I will this time. I'm ashamed of all the names I called you. Since I've known Zed all my life, I should have realized the exact same combination of an Adams and a Zohir couldn't be all bad.''

Talal smiled wryly. "So you've forgiven me?"

She nodded. "You've proved to me beyond the shadow of a doubt that long-lost brothers can be as lovable as well-known ones." Rising on her tiptoes, she kissed him first on one cheek, then the other. "Welcome to the family," she murmured.

Two and a half months later Talal, his cast finally off, returned in time to stand up as best man for Karen and Zed's wedding, creating a sensation among the guests. Since few of them had seen him, the remarkable resemblance startled many.

At the reception following the ceremony, Karen smiled when she overheard an older woman say to her husband, "All I can say is I hope she'll be able to tell one from the other when it comes time to take off for the honeymoon."

Zed looked down at her and grinned. "Think you can tell us apart?"

"For as long as he has to use that cane, anyway," she teased, positive that if Zed had a dozen clones she'd still be able to pick him out. "Danny isn't the only one who knows the difference."

As she said the words, she looked over at Talal, who was seated on a bench holding Danny. Ignoring the interested glances of more than one attractive woman guest, Talal dangled a brightly colored clown that balanced on a pole. The toy obviously fascinated Danny and Talal was completely preoccupied with the boy's reaction to the clown. Karen smiled to see how trustingly Danny cuddled against him.

Who said babies weren't good judges of character?

Epilogue

After a dry autumn, snow fell on December fifteenth, turning the brown fields of the Adams' ranch sparkling white. Standing at the kitchen window, Karen said, "I hope the snow stays until Christmas."

"More's on the way," Zed assured her. "You know this will be our second Christmas together, but our first Nevada one."

She nodded. "A real family Christmas this time. With my folks and brother Steve, plus Jade and Talal."

"Tal," Danny crowed, toddling across the kitchen, pulling behind him the wheeled camel Talal had sent him.

Karen turned to him. "Yes, Tal. Auntie Jade, too, and Uncle Steve."

Danny frowned, obviously unable to place Steve.

"Never mind," she told him. "It's been a while since the wedding so you've forgotten. You'll get to know Steve all over again after he gets here. And your grandparents."

"Tal," Danny repeated. He paused, turned around and patted the camel's head.

"Smartest kid in the universe," Zed remarked as he unhooked a banana from the holder and began peeling it.

"Nana," Danny said, dropping the string of the camel and making for Zed. "Me nana."

Zed broke off a chunk of banana and handed it to him. "You know," he said to Karen, "for a while there I thought Jade and Steve were going to hit it off. Maybe at Christmas...."

She shook her head. "I noticed some chemistry between them but nothing else. You need that elusive something else."

He crossed the kitchen and put his arms around her. "Want to show me about that something else?"

Karen smiled up at him. "Here and now? What will Danny think?"

"We can get started, anyway," Zed murmured, kissing her, long and slow and deep.

She snuggled closer, losing herself in his embrace even as she tried to calculate the hours until Danny's nap time. An insistent tugging at her skirt distracted her, causing her to break free and look down.

"Me kiss!" Danny insisted. "Me kiss."

Zed laughed ruefully, picked him up and kissed him. "If you keep interrupting, Tiger, you'll continue to be an only child."

Karen leaned over to kiss Danny, then whispered in Zed's ear, "Want to bet?"

* * * * *

Silhouette's newest series

YOURS TRULY

Love when you least expect it.

Where the written word plays a vital role in uniting couples—you're guaranteed a fun and exciting read every time!

Look for Marie Ferrarella's upcoming Yours Truly, *Traci on the Spot*, in March 1997.

Here's a special sneak preview....

1

---➤◄---

Morgan Brigham slowly set down his coffee cup on the kitchen table and stared at the comic strip in the center of his paper. It was nestled in among approximately twenty others that were spread out across two pages. But this was the only one he made a point of reading faithfully each morning at breakfast.

This was the only one that mirrored *her* life.

He read each panel twice, as if he couldn't trust his own eyes. But he could. It was there, in black and white.

Morgan folded the paper slowly, thoughtfully, his mind not on his task. So Traci was getting engaged.

The realization gnawed at the lining of his stomach. He hadn't a clue as to why.

He had even less of a clue why he did what he did next.

Abandoning his coffee, now cool, and the newspaper, and ignoring the fact that this was going to make him late for the office, Morgan went to get a sheet of stationery from the den.

He didn't have much time.

Traci Richardson stared at the last frame she had just drawn. Debating, she glanced at the creature sprawled out on the kitchen floor.

"What do you think, Jeremiah? Too blunt?"

The dog, part bloodhound, part mutt, idly looked up from his rawhide bone at the sound of his name. Jeremiah gave her a look she felt free to interpret as ambivalent.

"Fine help you are. What if Daniel actually reads this and puts two and two together?"

Not that there was all that much chance that the man who had proposed to her, the very prosperous and busy Dr. Daniel Thane, would actually see the comic strip she drew for a living. Not unless the strip was taped to a bicuspid he was examining. Lately Daniel had gotten so busy he'd stopped reading anything but the morning headlines of the *Times*.

Still, you never knew. "I don't want to hurt his feelings," Traci continued, using Jeremiah as a sounding board. "It's just that Traci is overwhelmed by Donald's proposal and, see, she thinks the ring is going to swallow her up." To prove her point, Traci held up the drawing for the dog to view.

This time, he didn't even bother to lift his head.

Traci stared moodily at the small velvet box on the kitchen counter. It had sat there since Daniel had asked her to marry him last Sunday. Even if Daniel never read her comic strip, he was going to suspect something eventually. The very fact that she hadn't grabbed the ring from his hand and slid it onto her finger should have told him that she had doubts about their union.

Traci sighed. Daniel was a catch by any definition. So what was her problem? She kept waiting to be struck by that sunny ray of happiness. Daniel said he wanted to take care of her, to fulfill her every wish. And he was even willing to let her think about it before she gave him her answer.

Guilt nibbled at her. She should be dancing up and down, not wavering like a weather vane in a gale.

Pronouncing the strip completed, she scribbled her signature in the corner of the last frame and then sighed. Another week's work put to bed. She glanced at the pile of mail on the counter. She'd been bringing it in steadily from the mailbox since Monday, but the stack had gotten no farther than her kitchen. Sorting letters seemed the least heinous of all the annoying chores that faced her.

Traci paused as she noted a long envelope. Morgan Brigham. Why would Morgan be writing to her?

Curious, she tore open the envelope and quickly scanned the short note inside.

Dear Traci,

I'm putting the summerhouse up for sale. Thought you might want to come up and see it one more time before it goes up on the block. Or make a bid for it yourself. If memory serves, you once said you wanted to buy it. Either way, let me know. My number's on the card.

Take care,
Morgan

P.S. Got a kick out of *Traci on the Spot* this week.

Traci folded the letter. He read her strip. She hadn't known that. A feeling of pride silently coaxed a smile to her lips. After a beat, though, the rest of his note seeped into her consciousness. He was selling the house.

The summerhouse. A faded white building with brick trim. Suddenly, memories flooded her mind. Long, lazy afternoons that felt as if they would never end.

Morgan.

She looked at the far wall in the family room. There was a large framed photograph of her and Morgan standing before the summerhouse. Traci and Morgan. Morgan and Traci. Back then, it seemed their lives had been permanently intertwined. A bittersweet feeling of loss passed over her.

Traci quickly pulled the telephone over to her on the counter and tapped out the number on the keypad.

*   *   *   *   *

*Look for TRACI ON THE SPOT
by Marie Ferrarella, coming to
Silhouette YOURS TRULY
in March 1997.*

FORTUNE'S Children™

Bestselling Author

CHRISTINE RIMMER

Continues the twelve-book series—FORTUNE'S CHILDREN—
in February 1997 with Book Eight

WIFE WANTED

The last thing schoolteacher Natalie Fortune wanted was
to fall for her new tenant—sexy, single father Eric Dalton.
The man needed lessons in child rearing! But when an
accident forced her to rely on Eric's help, Natalie found
herself wishing his loving care would last a lifetime.

MEET THE FORTUNES—a family whose legacy is greater than
riches. Because where there's a will...there's a *wedding!*

FC-8

Silhouette®

SPECIAL ▼ EDITION™

COMING NEXT MONTH

*If you're looking for irresistible
heroes, the search is over....*

Joan Elliott Pickart's

Tux, Bram and Blue Bishop and their pal,
Gibson McKinley, are four unforgettable men...on a
wife hunt. Discover the women who steal their
Texas-size hearts in this enchanting four-book series,
which alternates between Silhouette Desire
and Special Edition:

In February 1997, fall in love with Tux, Desire's
Man of the Month, in **TEXAS MOON,** #1051.

In May 1997, Blue meets his match in **TEXAS DAWN,**
Special Edition #1100.

In August 1997, don't miss Bram's romance in
TEXAS GLORY—coming to you from Desire.

And in December 1997, Gib takes more than marriage
vows in **TEXAS BABY,** Special Edition's
That's My Baby! title.
You won't be able to resist
Joan Elliott Pickart's **TEXAS BABY.**

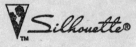

Harlequin and Silhouette celebrate
Black History Month with seven terrific titles,
featuring the all-new *Fever Rising*
by Maggie Ferguson
(Harlequin Intrigue #408) and
A Family Wedding by Angela Benson
(Silhouette Special Edition #1085)!

Also available are:
Looks Are Deceiving by Maggie Ferguson
Crime of Passion by Maggie Ferguson
Adam and Eva by Sandra Kitt
Unforgivable by Joyce McGill
Blood Sympathy by Reginald Hill

On sale in January at your favorite
Harlequin and Silhouette retail outlet.

Look us up on-line at: http://www.romance.net   BHM297